Praise for *Jacob's Bell*

"*Jacob's Bell*, by John Snyder, is a splendid achievement and 'rings' with many truths. Snyder cares about his characters and makes us come to care as well. He gives us Jacob McCallum, a man who had it all until his addiction to alcohol took everything away and he lost his fortune, his family, and his way in life. Snyder writes with simplicity and depth about the harshness and vagaries that life can bring but also about its beauty. He shows a reverence for the past and memories that may be from years ago but which are given as fresh and as near as this minute. His prose resounds with a love of people and the world and is grounded in the particulars of our America—its cities and byways, its taverns and highways. *Jacob's Bell* is a book that has, in my judgment, exceptional merit. It registers the redemptive power of forgiveness and love, and I highly recommend it."

—*Brian Avery, film producer, Yari Film Group—Los Angeles, CA*

"*Jacob's Bell* takes readers on a journey of success and failure, love and hate, bitterness and repentance. This tale promises to become a Christmas classic that transports each of us to many familiar and unfamiliar places, all the while calling us to a place of forgiveness and restoration. *Jacob's Bell* is a gift that reminds us of the TRUE meaning of Christmas and the forgiveness that comes when we trust in God's indescribable gift…his Son Jesus. *Jacob's Bell* will hold a special place in our family library and Christmas tradition!"

—*Jeff Sheets, former president, Echolight Studios, Franklin, TN*

"I was so moved by John Snyder's latest book, *Jacob's Bell*. It reminded me of God's blessings in our lives and how there is nothing more important than generosity, family, faith, and forgiveness. With these things, the impossible becomes possible. John has reminded us why Christmas is so special, and I am truly blessed to have read this remarkable story. Amen."

—*Dan Angel, film producer and president, Fezziwig Studios, Los Angeles, CA*

"John has once again written a gem of a book. He is able to highlight spirituality without excessive sentimentality. I heartily recommend it to anyone who would like to be inspired and entertained by good writing."

—*Bob Parsley, pastor, First Baptist Church of Crofton, Maryland*

Praise for *The Golden Ring*

"I read a lot of fiction, particularly Christian fiction. And I enjoy novellas, particularly Christmas stories. Having read scores of them over the past decade or so, I can say without reservation that in every regard—style, story, substance—*The Golden Ring* merits a place on the Christmas Classics shelf right alongside *A Christmas Carol*, *The Other Wise Man* and more contemporary bestsellers [such as] VanLiere's *The Christmas Shoes* or Richard Paul Evans's *The Christmas Box*."

—*Randall Murphree, Editor, American Family Association*

"A new book published last year must be added to your collection and given as gifts. *The Golden Ring* by John Snyder is destined

to become a classic that will be read chapter by chapter by anyone who wants to get closer to the essence of Christmas."
—*Jill Kamp, The Washington Times, Washington, DC*

"*The Golden Ring* is not only a meaningful gift for those you love, but will also serve as a catalyst for giving and receiving your own family stories. What better package to place under the tree?"
—*Jamie Whitfield, BookPage*

"Here is a story that deals with the real meaning of Christmas. This is the kind of story that you could sit around with the entire family and read. It's very entertaining—very heartwarming."
—*Doug Griffith, WAYM-FM, Nashville, TN*

"What started out as a simple conversation over a cup of coffee between a grandson and his grandmother turned into a Christmas story that pulls on the heartstrings and stirs emotions that readers may not have known existed.... For a gift for someone special, no matter what age, or a gift to warm the heart, touch the senses and travel to a place never seen before..."
—*Thomas Dennison, The Enquirer Gazette, Upper Marlboro, MD*

"It was Snyder's curiosity that led him to question Anna Snyder. It was intrigue which led to the investigation of her biographical and historical recounts. But it was the writer in Snyder which allowed him to combine loving memories with factual information and comprise a loving, warm Christmas book which can warm the heart on a chilly day this holiday season."
—*Barbara Bolden, Managing Editor,*
The Prince George's Sentinel, Lanham, MD

ALSO BY JOHN SNYDER

The Golden Ring: A Christmas Story

JACOB'S BELL

A Christmas Story

JOHN SNYDER

Nashville New York

FaithWords
Hachette Book Group
1290 Avenue of the Americas, New York, NY 10104
faithwords.com
twitter.com/faithwords

First Edition: October 2018

FaithWords is a division of Hachette Book Group, Inc. The FaithWords name and logo are trademarks of Hachette Book Group, Inc.

The publisher is not responsible for websites (or their content) that are not owned by the publisher.

The Hachette Speakers Bureau provides a wide range of authors for speaking events. To find out more, go to www.hachettespeakersbureau.com or call (866) 376-6591.

Library of Congress Cataloging-in-Publication Data has been applied for.

ISBNs: 978-1-5460-1039-5 (paper over board), 978-1-5460-1041-8 (ebook)

Printed in the United States of America

LSC-C

10 9 8 7 6 5 4 3 2 1

To the many Salvation Army Bell Ringers who weather the elements during the Christmas season each year to ring in the holiday and help facilitate a better way of life for millions of people in need.

Chapter One

A deafening screech, then a loud thud jolted Jacob McCallum upright from his slumber as the freight train pulled into the Chicago yards on a chilly September morning in 1944. The boxcar, which carried him from the West, had a musty stench about it. Jacob's head throbbed. His breath reeked of whiskey and tobacco. An empty whiskey bottle lay next to his right leg—the remnants of a hard night's drinking. He lay his head back down on his knapsack and lit the stub of a cigarette as he watched the sunlight trickle through the cracks into the emptiness of the darkened wooden boxcar. Accustomed to traveling this way, he journeyed across the country looking for odd jobs and handouts to support himself.

As the train slowed, Jacob prepared to jump off. It wasn't wise to linger after the train pulled into the yard. Though hopping a freight wasn't a serious crime, they *were* cracking down. If caught, he could be arrested.

Jacob slid the door open and squinted hard as the bright morning sun reflected off his face. Instinctively, his right hand rose to his face, shielding his eyes while they adjusted to the light. The sun revealed the weathered skin of a sixty-three-year-old man who appeared much older, the cumulative result from many years of hard living on the streets. Jacob lived a callous life and carried the scars to prove it. Over the years, his face and head wore more stitches than a fine country quilt from countless fights, falls, and knocks to the skull.

The son of Irish immigrants, Jacob grew up on the south side of Chicago, a notoriously tough neighborhood. The skills he learned as a lad with his knuckles proved handy over the years, getting him out of plenty of tight spots, and *into* just as many. He spent most of his time riding the rails and hanging out on the streets with roughnecks and hooligans. His fighting skills were honed in prison, where he fought for recreation and for the amusement of the guards. Mostly, though, his fighting, just like his drinking, got him into trouble more than anything else.

Like the time when he was just thirteen and he came upon his older brother cornered by two adult thugs trying to strong-arm him for his billfold. His brother was sixteen at the time, but far more timid than Jacob. Backed against an alley wall, he pleaded with his robbers to let him go. Jacob snuck up from behind, introducing himself with a sucker punch out of left field, knocking one of the ruffians down. To even his chances, he snatched a heavy metal pipe from the ground and cracked it hard over the knee caps of the other before chasing both of them down the alley, wildly swinging the pipe over his head as he ran. As the trio rounded the corner, they rushed directly into a group of the muggers' friends, who promptly came to their aid, issuing Jacob a mighty beating. His brother, unaware, safely made his escape, only to witness Jacob's return home bloodied and bruised.

Jacob jumped from the boxcar as it slowly rolled into the yard. He executed a perfect landing. Standing there proudly, he puckered his lips and drew one last time on what was left of his cigarette, savoring the last of its nicotine. Tossing the smoldering butt onto the tracks, he rubbed his hand over his unshaven face, where a white stubble had emerged. *I'm gettin' too old for this nonsense,* he thought to himself as he walked across the train yard. Jumping freight trains, sleeping on the ground, and enduring the elements didn't come as easily as they used to.

He hadn't always lived this way. Jacob *did* have three grown children. Emma, his eldest, lived somewhere in Baltimore, Maryland. Frankie, the youngest, lived with his older brother, Tom, and his family in Chicago—the last Jacob had heard. Tom and Frankie were the motives for Jacob's visit to the city. He needed to put things right between himself and his two sons. Jacob had been riddled with guilt over the years for the tragedy he'd brought upon his older son, evidenced by a limp Tom would have the rest of his life.

A recent near-death experience out West spurred Jacob to take an accounting of his life. He came down with a bad bout of pneumonia and almost didn't make it. While lying in a hospital bed in Nevada, he came to the realization he needed to reconcile with his children before his time ran out.

Five years had passed since he had last seen his sons, even longer since he had seen Emma. He hadn't seen his granddaughter since she was a baby. Emma made sure of that. He had yet to meet Tom's young son, Michael, who was born three years earlier. Jacob's relationship with his children was chilly at best. And it took years just to reach that level of warmth. Tom's parting words from Jacob's last visit still echoed in his head.

"Now get out of here and never come back again!" His encounters with Emma had a similar history. Jacob's family wanted little to do with him, and for good reason.

As he made his way through the streets of Chicago, he noticed there were not many young men about, and the ones that were wore uniforms. World War II was in full fury. Most of the young men of Chicago, like young men in every other city and town in America, were being consumed by the global war. He wondered about Frankie—was he, too, wearing a uniform?

Jacob often pondered about his youngest child. He knew Tom and Emma were fine. They were strong, sometimes even stubborn, much like him. But Frankie was different, more like his mother, sensitive and overly generous, far less independent than his siblings. The turmoil Jacob had brought upon his family seemed to have a more profound effect on Frankie, but in a quiet sort of way. He never lost his temper or showed anger toward Jacob as did Tom and Emma. Frankie always seemed less emotional, more withdrawn. But Jacob knew that what he had done had deeply scarred his youngest child. Through it all, though, Frankie seemed to show Jacob more love and respect than his siblings.

Jacob projected a tough exterior, walking with a cocky gait, but on the inside he was hurting. Haunted by memories of the past, filled with regrets and what-ifs, he longed for love and companionship, which had evaded him for so many years. For most of the last two decades, Jacob existed in an alcohol-induced fog, a time of denial and self-pity mixed with intermittent periods of remorse, sobriety, and attempts at reconciliation.

Jacob stopped, slung his coat over his shoulder, and inserted a crumpled cigarette into the corner of his mouth.

"Got a light?" he asked a passerby.

"Sure, pal."

Jacob leaned his head into the palms of the stranger's hands as they cupped the matchstick. Drawing the flame onto the end of his cigarette, he stood upright and inhaled deeply.

While exhaling, he asked, "Know a place where a fella can get a drink this early?"

"Down the street, turn the corner, and at the end of the block is a joint called Kelly's."

"Thanks."

Jacob headed to Kelly's for a morning fix of liquid courage before he would begin his quest to find his sons and attempt to extinguish the burning in his heart. As he strolled through the warehouse district of the city, his memory took him back to a distant time, some thirty years before. Dressed in an expensive suit partially hidden by a fashionable woolen topcoat, he wore freshly shined shoes made of expensive Italian leather, and his hair was full and slicked back in a way that accentuated his chiseled features and a strong jawline, features that attracted the attention of the ladies when he walked by. Surrounded by associates, he was greeted warmly by passersby, who regarded him with much respect. After all, he *was* among the richest and most powerful men in Chicago.

"Hey, old man, watch where you're going!"

Startled back into the present when he bumped shoulders with a man on the sidewalk, Jacob passively let the encounter go without incident. In his younger day, the guy's rude remark most likely would have put him on the receiving end of one of Jacob's well-established right hooks. But ol' Jacob was tired, tired of fighting, tired of running—just plain ol' tired. He offered a muted apology: "Sorry. I wasn't paying attention."

"Well, why don't you watch where you're going?"

"I said I was sorry."

The confrontation caused Jacob to drop his coat onto the ground. He stared down at the pathetic piece of cloth, riddled with holes, the pockets ripped at the sides. Honestly, it wasn't worth the effort to bend over and pick it up, but it was all Jacob had, a far cry from the fine woolen topcoat he once wore.

Spotting the sign over the front door, he stopped in front of Kelly's. Flicking his spent cigarette out into the street, he opened the door and walked inside. The place was practically empty. The barkeep, chewing on a half-smoked cigar, was sweeping the floor. Five shabbily dressed patrons were seated at a table playing poker, and in the corner a guy slept soundly in a booth, his head resting on the table in front of him. The place smelled of stale beer and cigarette smoke. The glow of the morning sun, which snuck through the pub's smoggy windows, provided the only light in the dim establishment. It flowed into the smoke-filled room, its beams of light spilling onto the dirty wooden floor.

Jacob pulled out a stool and bellied up to the bar. The bartender disregarded him and just kept sweeping. He sat patiently for a few moments before becoming irritated at being ignored.

"Hey, buddy!" Jacob called out.

Still, the bartender kept sweeping.

"Hey, buddy. I'm talking to you."

The bartender looked up and said, "I'm not your buddy."

"Well, I'd like a drink. You *are* the bartender, aren't you?"

Without answering, the man walked behind the bar, stopped across from Jacob, leaned in, and said, "What'll ya have?"

"A tall glass of whiskey."

The bartender poured whiskey into a dirty glass and put it on the bar in front of Jacob. As Jacob reached for it, the man pulled it back.

"You pay first, *then* you drink."

Jacob rummaged through his pockets for the price of the booze. Finding it, he slapped it down on the bar. The bartender released his grip on the glass, grabbed the money, and slid the drink toward Jacob. *Friendly place*, Jacob thought.

As he straddled the bar stool sipping his whiskey, Jacob eavesdropped on the men playing cards as they cursed loudly and laughed at the punch lines of off-color jokes. He grabbed a box of matches sitting on the bar and fumbled through his pockets for a smoke. Searching frantically, he checked his pants, his shirt, his sweater, and his coat—nothing. He was out. He could bum a smoke from one of the guys playing cards. But that could lead to trouble.

He craned his neck in the bartender's direction, who was busily wiping off some tables behind him. Out of the question. Then, he glanced at the man sleeping in the corner booth. Sitting on the table by his elbow sat half a pack of Lucky Strikes, Jacob's preferred brand, but these days he wasn't too particular. *I could sneak over and snag the pack. The dope probably wouldn't even notice. A smoke sure would go good with this whiskey.*

Jacob redirected his roving eyes down to his feet. *This must be my lucky day*, he laughed inwardly. There, just below the bar, lay a long cigarette butt. Someone had discarded it after taking just a few drags, prematurely snuffing it out on the floor. Fortunately for Jacob, the bartender wasn't that conscientious about his cleaning. He bent over and lifted the castoff to his lips. Lighting it, he smiled, then turned his attention to the drink he had been neglecting.

His thoughts returned to his past, to happier times, like the day more than thirty years before, when he and Nick, his best friend and business partner, made that big deal. *Wow...we sure were flying high that day. We really hit the jackpot.* A slight smile crept onto his face, then quickly disappeared. *Yeah...and where did all that get me in the end? Where I am today...in a run-down bar sniping cigarette butts off the floor.*

Whatever became of Nick? he wondered. *He's got to be doing better than me.* He dreamed of the beautiful home he once owned. Some called it a mansion. He drove fancy cars and wore imported suits with silk shirts and ties.

Looking down at his clothes, he frowned at seeing how they were all tattered and torn, pants with patches. His shoes were customized with stuffed cardboard inserts to cover the holes in their soles. He laughed out loud, then joked to himself, *I've got holes in my soles and a hole in my soul.* All of a sudden, it wasn't funny anymore. He *did* have a hole in his soul, and it ached.

How could my life have turned like this? I had it all—everything. Now I have nothing...no money, no home, no fancy cars, and most importantly, no family. Nothing!

Of all the things he missed, he longed for his family the most. But he knew that part of his life he could never recapture. Jacob took another swig of whiskey and swallowed hard. He puffed on his cigarette and blew out a ring of smoke, watching it glide toward the ceiling, where it disappeared in the slow whirling blades of the ceiling fan. As he gazed upward, his thoughts again drifted back to his past.

He and Nick went way back—all the way back to their childhood. Nick introduced Jacob to his wife, Amanda, a moment which Jacob would always remember. She was stunningly beautiful with her pale blond hair and blue eyes. They fell deeply in love... a love that still caused Jacob deep anguish.

I should have listened to Nick. My life would be far different today if I had.

"Ouch, dang it!" Jacob's cigarette burned down to his fingers. His yell caused the men playing cards to turn and stare. The bartender dropped the glass he was washing, and the gentleman sleeping in the corner began to stir. Jacob kept his head down, avoiding eye contact, acting as if his indiscretion had never happened. After stubbing out the cigarette, he tilted his head back and poured the remaining whiskey down his throat before confidently slamming the glass back on the bar, picking up his coat, and walking out the door.

The light of the outdoors glared in his eyes. He staggered slightly for a brief moment, partially because of the gleaming sun, but mostly because of the whiskey he'd consumed. He plopped down on a bench in front of the building. A few minutes later, the front door of Kelly's swung open and the man who had been sleeping in the corner emerged.

"Hey, mate," the disheveled gentleman said with a prominent British accent. "Mind if I sit here a spell?" He lit one of his Lucky Strikes. "Care for a smoke?"

Ah... that was music to Jacob's ears.

"Sure. Don't mind if I do."

"I haven't seen you around here before. You from Chicago?"

"Originally. But I've been gone for a while," Jacob said. "Just passing through. I'm here to see my sons. How about you?"

"I rent a room down the street. It isn't much, but it's a warm place to bunk. Would you care for a nip?" the British gent said as he pulled a bottle of scotch from inside his coat.

"No. I've got to be going. Gotta get to my sons' place."

"Oh, come on, mate. A few nips on the bottle will warm you up inside."

Jacob thought for a moment. He wanted to find Tom and Frankie to straighten things out...to say the things he came there to say. But his fear of Tom's rejection gave Jacob a reason to kill some time with his new friend. After all, Jacob had robbed his children of their mother's life, and he knew this would always be a barrier to a meaningful relationship with them. Painfully, he realized that Tom's feelings of disdain toward him were justified.

"Maybe just a few nips, then I have to go."

Actually, the gentleman's offer enticed Jacob to put off his plans...more appealing than sure rejection. A kind stranger willing to share a bottle of scotch and his Lucky Strikes offered the perfect reason to put off his meeting with Tom and Frankie. He spent several hours with his newfound friend, long enough to help find the bottom of the bottle of scotch and to empty that pack of Lucky Strikes. After bidding the man good-bye, Jacob staggered down the street and into another bar, where he stayed much too long.

Chapter Two

As Tom walked up the street, images of his father came into his mind with every step he took, his limp a poignant keepsake of his father's recklessness. His recollection of the man oozed like an open wound. All his life, Tom had struggled with the scars left behind by his father. He tried hard to remember the good times he'd experienced as a child, the times he'd gone fishing and attended ball games with his dad, but these memories were overshadowed by his father's drinking, carousing, and bad judgment.

Tom and his siblings had been raised by his mother's brother, Uncle Phil, and his wife, Aunt Mildred, while Jacob remained incarcerated. Growing up with relatives, Tom could never remember anything good ever being said about his father. He often made a conscious effort to block even the good memories of him. Missing his mother, though, he yearned for just a whiff of her sweet perfume or the gentle touch of her soft hands. What a wonderful woman. He could only imagine what it would be like to have her in his life.

Though taller than his father, Tom favored him remark-ably, especially in his younger years, handsome and muscular. He married his childhood sweetheart, Betty Matthews, and they were the proud parents of a small child, Michael, age three. A devoted family man, Tom loved fatherhood and made a concerted effort to spend as much time with Michael as possible.

He shared a good relationship with his siblings, especially with Frankie. In many ways, Tom shouldered more of a father's role with Frankie than that of a brother. Before entering the Army and being shipped out to Europe for the war, Frankie had lived with Tom and Betty. Never really living on his own, he re-lied on Tom for guidance and support.

Tom arrived at work a few minutes late, something he pawned off on his lame leg, another thing for which he could blame his father. He worked in a machine shop as a skilled machinist. His impressive work ethic made him the perfect employee and well liked, but the lack of opportunity for ad-vancement in the small shop frustrated him. Being short on seniority further inhibited his prospects. He yearned to own a business, but lacked the self-confidence, not to mention the fi-nancial resources, for such a venture. So he settled for being a dedicated underling.

At lunchtime, Tom walked outside and ate at the picnic table behind the shop. The afternoon sun warmed the chill in the air. He preferred the solitude of eating his lunch alone. It afforded him the opportunity to think about his life. Before lifting his sandwich to his mouth, he bowed his head for a short prayer. While chewing his first bite, he began thinking about his son. Last weekend they'd gone to the park and done a little fishing.

The fish weren't biting so he and Michael walked around the lake, enjoying their time together.

This prompted a memory of one particular Saturday afternoon when he was a young boy. His father took him fishing. Tom caught all of the fish and his father didn't catch any. He thought that was great—out-fishing the old man. He later learned that his father was fishing without bait, letting Tom win the bragging rights for the day. That's the kind of dad Jacob was in the earlier years, unselfish and tremendously thoughtful. It brought a slight smile to Tom's face.

In some ways, Tom was conflicted about his feelings for his father because he had some great memories. But then Jacob changed. He became selfish and hard, spending less and less time with the family and more time carousing and drinking with his no-good friends.

I wish things had turned out different, he thought. *I would love to have a relationship with Dad. And Michael would have love having a grandfather . . . if only he hadn't changed so.*

Tom occasionally wondered if his father could ever revert back to the man he used to be. After these many years, he doubted it. But to be honest, he never really gave Jacob a chance, too afraid to open his heart, only to have it smashed once again.

About five years earlier, Jacob had actually showed up and asked for a fresh start with him and Frankie—fat chance, as far as Tom was concerned. He told him he'd missed his chance and slammed the door in his face. His father had fooled him before with promises that he'd changed, only to go back to being an irresponsible drunk. Never again would Tom fall for that line. Part of him knew this was wrong. As a Christian man, he realized the importance of forgiveness in his faith. When he sought the advice of his pastor and friends, they told him he should, at least, give his father an opportunity to apologize and see where it went from there. But like his father, Tom had a stubborn streak.

Five o'clock came fast. As Tom packed up his things to go home, Randy Fleming, his best friend and co-worker, approached him.

"Me and some of the boys are stopping off at Mattie's Pub for a beer or two on the way home. Want to join us?"

"I don't know," Tom said. "Betty's expecting me."

"Oh, come on, Tom. We won't be late. Have a beer and a few laughs with us."

Tom thought for a moment, then agreed to go. Once there his somber mood lifted as he joked with his friends. They began throwing darts, a game at which Tom excelled. After beating his friend, he and Randy returned to their table and let some other guys have their turn.

"How's Virginia and little Billy?" Tom asked.

"Oh, they're doing fine. Billy's really a pistol, though. He's so excited about the prospect of having a little brother or sister."

"Well, at least he doesn't have long to wait. Virginia's due anytime now, isn't she?"

Randy nodded and took a drink of beer. "It's about time for you and Betty to start thinking about a little playmate for Michael, ain't it?"

"Not on my wages. It's all I can do to put bread on the table as things are now."

Suddenly, Tom's attention focused on a drunkard at the corner table fumbling for a cigarette, swaying unsteadily in his seat. People were laughing at the man as he tried to light his smoke.

Randy noticed Tom staring at the man, watching his expression change from one of happiness to pain. He knew what he was thinking. He let Tom sit silently for a moment before saying, "Thinking about your father, aren't you?"

"Yeah. That's what he's probably doing right now, wherever he is—dead drunk and making a fool of himself."

"What if he's changed?"

"Oh, not to worry—he hasn't."

"You don't know that, Tom. He's getting up in years. He may have changed his ways. It's been a while since you've seen him. I know you think about him."

"I try not to."

"Come on, Tom. He's your father."

"He's a disgrace."

"What if he showed up one day and told you he's changed?"

"I'd probably pitch him out like I've done before."

"You wouldn't give him a chance?"

"No! Can we change the subject?" Tom said, raising his voice. "Whose side are you on anyway?"

Randy let it drop.

"Let me get us another round," Randy offered.

Tom's eyes turned back to the drunk. "No, this is it for me."

Tom had a healthy respect for alcohol. He usually stopped at one or two drinks, swearing he would never be an alcoholic like his father.

He stayed another five minutes, took the last swig of his beer, then grabbed his coat and headed out the front door of the bar. On the way home he couldn't stop thinking about the drunk in the corner. It made him wonder about his father and what he might be doing.

Upon arriving home, Michael, his toddler son, ran up to greet him. Tom stooped to pick him up, then kissed Betty. She was beautiful...small boned, sharing many of the same qualities as Tom's mother: kind, warm, and pleasant to be around.

"How was your day, dear?"

"It was good. I stopped by Mattie's with Randy and some of the guys after work for a beer."

"I wondered what was taking you so long to get home."

"You're not angry, are you?"

"Oh, no. You deserve time with your friends. How's Randy doing? Any news about the baby?"

"He's doing great. Said the baby's due anytime now."

"That's wonderful. Now little Billy will have a playmate."

"Yeah, if it's another son...that will be twice the trouble." He laughed. "I'm starved; what's for supper?"

"I fixed a meatloaf. Let me put Michael to bed and then we'll eat."

Tom took a seat at the table and began thumbing through the newspaper while Betty attended to Michael. The alluring smell of the meatloaf stole his attention. He walked over to the stove, opened the oven door, and inhaled deeply, taking in an unfiltered scent of the dish. Snatching a fork, he bent over the meatloaf, carefully guiding the utensil toward its target.

"Ah-hum," Betty interrupted.

"Oh...I was just checking it."

"Sure you were." She laughed.

"All right...You caught me red-handed."

"Sit down and I'll get you a slice in a minute. Do you want mashed potatoes to go with it?"

"What do you think?"

"I thought you would."

Betty cut off a generous slab of meatloaf and spooned up an extra helping of mashed potatoes, Tom's favorite. She set the plate in front of him, then fixed a plate for herself before taking her place at the table. They graciously bowed their heads as Tom said the blessing.

"Tom, I was thinking today...Do you ever wish your relationship with your father was better?"

"What made you ask that question?"

"Oh, I don't know, I just think it would be nice for Michael to have his grandfather in his life, especially since my daddy's gone."

"What's with everybody today...all worried about me and my relationship with my father?"

"What do you mean, Tom?"

"Randy got on me about the same thing at the pub."

"About your father?"

"Oh, never mind! Let's just drop it!"

"I'm sorry, dear. I didn't mean to upset you."

She placed her hands on his to comfort him.

"Look, it just isn't within me to forgive him. Not right now anyway."

"It *is* within your power to forgive. I know he has his faults, but don't you think it would be good for Michael to know his grandfather?"

"Are you kidding me? I don't want my son anywhere near that man. He's a terrible influence."

"What if he's changed?"

"You're talking about the impossible."

"Miracles happen, you know."

"Now that *would* be a miracle."

"It's certainly a dream of mine."

"You know the havoc he's brought upon me and my family. I would prefer to keep Michael out of my father's wake of destruction. Let's talk about something more pleasant."

"Such as?"

"Such as how beautiful you are."

Betty smiled.

"Especially when you smile."

"It's been a while since you spoke with Emma."

"I received a letter from her a few days ago."

"What did she have to say?"

"Everything's fine in Baltimore. She said she got a letter from Frankie."

"We got one today, too. I forgot to tell you."

"Where is it?"

"Here, I'll get it for you."

Betty jumped up from the table and retrieved the letter. Setting it down by Tom's plate, she said, "Read it out loud, will you, please?"

Tom put down his fork. Using his knife, he opened the letter.

Dear Tom and Betty,

I thought I'd write to let you know I'm okay. It is cold over here. Snowed today a little bit. I know I've been out of touch for a while, but the Germans keep us pretty busy. Yesterday we kicked their butts in a battle. Two of my buddies were wounded . . . not badly, but they'll be out of commission for a while. I'm trying to keep my head down. Maybe this thing will be over soon, but there doesn't seem like there's an end in sight. How's my little Michael? I'll bet he is growing up fast. I'd love to give him a big hug right now. You know, Tom...I would love for Dad to see me in my uniform. I think he'd be proud of me. I know how you feel about him, but my time over here has made me do a lot of thinking. I'd really like to see him. When I get back, do you think we could work on that? Think about it, will you? I'll write again as soon as possible. We have a mission tomorrow, and then I'll be off for a few days. I'll write then. I love you both.

—Frankie

As he gently placed the letter down on the table, an empty stare occupied Tom's face. Betty put her hands on his again. A tear rolled down his cheek.

"Maybe God is trying to tell me something...about Dad, I mean."

"Maybe. Do you think he's all right?"

"I have no idea."

"I'm worried about him, Tom."

"Don't waste your time worrying about him."

"Tom!"

Chapter Three

Frankie and his fellow soldiers had just settled in when word came down that the Germans had broken through the line and were still coming. Frankie's division, among others, stood by waiting to mount a counterattack. Soon, their orders came to proceed ahead to the front line and to prepare for combat.

They traveled light, one blanket, one gun, and one knapsack per man. The route to the front line was entangled with Germans, the going exceedingly tough as casualties mounted. Frankie walked cautiously, carrying his gun at the ready. Many of his comrades who walked with him fell wounded and dead, and they were still miles from the front, where the combat was *supposed* to begin. This was not a drill, not a training exercise, but the real deal ... war and all its horror.

Artillery explosions peppered the night sky, lighting the heavens in what seemed like a fireworks display. Frankie's heart raced as he wondered when his number would come up. He walked, then began running. The men regrouped from time to time, those who were still standing.

When they finally arrived at the front line, Frankie thought he had seen it all, but none of his training had prepared him for this. There were American soldiers dying all around him, artillery shells exploding everywhere, the screams, the smells, the ear-piercing noise...nothing but confusion and chaos. Some men ducked for cover, while other brave souls charged ahead firing their weapons. It was as if he wasn't even there—just watching it all happen from a distance. It all seemed like a dream...a bloodcurdling nightmare, in fact. Terribly frightened, Frankie did his best to fight through it.

A sergeant yelled, "Soldiers! You, you, and you...take this machine gun up that hill where you'll have a vantage point and take out some of these Krauts. They're killing us here!"

Frankie obeyed the order, following two men he didn't even know to a place he never wanted to go. Once at the top of the hill, they set up the gun. By the flickering lights in the sky, one soldier pointed out the Germans, the other manned the ammo, and Frankie took out as many "Krauts" as he could...just like he was ordered. The enemy dropped by the dozens, but they kept coming.

He mowed down another group. One man got through and started charging toward them. Frankie took aim, but hesitated for a second while the thought flashed through his head that this was another human being. *What am I doing?*

"Shoot him!" a soldier shouted.

Frankie pulled the trigger again as a shower of bullets sprayed from the gun's barrel, hitting the rogue German soldier, knocking him to the ground.

"He's not dead. Shoot him again!"

The German struggled to his feet and pulled a grenade from

his belt. Wounded, he staggered toward them. Frankie could see his face, which reflected the same fear as his own. Confronted with no other alternative, he fired again. The bullets exploded against the young man's chest and he fell—dead.

Suddenly, the gun jammed. Frankie tried to dislodge the shell casing that was wedged in the magazine. They were pinned down and taking a constant barrage of bullets. The Germans advanced and were overrunning them. Retreat being their only chance for survival, Frankie picked up the machine gun and they all ran just as fast as they could. The weight of the gun became a hindrance, so they made the impulsive decision to drop it to hasten their flight, while bullets whizzed by their heads and into the bushes around them. Frankie ran for about a mile until he caught up to some of the division. When he turned around, he discovered that he was alone. The other two men were taken by enemy fire, all before Frankie was even able to introduce himself.

The refuge Frankie sought was short lived. A soldier handed him another rifle and told him to fall in line. It would be a long night, but he successfully survived another scrape with death.

Early the next morning, Frankie began writing Emma a letter. He couldn't stop thinking about the German soldier he'd killed...the look in his eyes. All of a sudden he felt sick to his stomach. He climbed out of the foxhole on his hands and knees, succumbing to a case of the dry heaves.

"God, forgive me. Please, forgive me."

He knelt there shaking for almost five minutes before he could regain his composure. A sergeant, who saw the whole thing, yelled over to him, "Buck up, soldier!" Frankie wiped his mouth with the sleeve of his jacket before returning to his foxhole and resuming his letter to Emma.

★ ★ ★

Dear Sis,

I thought I'd write you a brief note while I had the chance. We were in a horrible battle last night. I wish I could say it was exciting, but it wasn't. It was downright scary and I'm not embarrassed to admit it. I had several friends die and many that I fought next to that I never got to know. I did a terrible thing last night. I killed many men. One, in particular, still haunts me. I can still see his face as I shot him over and over again. I hate this. I'm just not cut out for killing. We're waiting for our orders. Who knows where they'll send us next. I just wanted to let you know I was safe—relatively speaking. I will write again when I get the chance. If you talk to Tom, tell him I'm waiting for a letter from him. Take good care of yourself.

Love, Frankie

Tears of worry welled in Emma's eyes as she read the letter. She wished Frankie could come home, that all the men could come back to America and be safe. The thought that the entire world was at war seriously disturbed her.

She pulled her daughter next to her and held her close.

"Is Uncle Frankie okay, Mommy?"

"He's fine, dear. He's fine."

Chapter Four

Jacob awakened to someone kicking his feet. As he strained his eyes against the bright morning sun, his sight was hazy. Once he'd focused, the image became clearer. He made out the shadow of a large man hovering over him, his eyes zeroing in on a brass belt buckle and a badge, and then to the billy club the man was slapping repeatedly into his open palm. An imposing figure and definitely impressed by his own authority, the cop peered down upon him. He stood erect, his legs spread slightly apart, his face wrinkled and his lips pursed, with a service revolver hanging loose at his side, as if he were a gun slinger from the Wild, Wild West.

"Hey, you! Wake up and beat it, or I'll run you in."

Jacob bolted upright, rubbing his face. He removed the blanket of newspapers and cardboard that had covered him during his drunken night on the street. As he stood, he became unsteady on his feet, leaning against the wall of the building near him for support.

"What makes you think you can just lay down and sleep off your drunk wherever you want?"

Jacob grasped for a plausible explanation. "Well, sir...I just...ah..."

"Stand up straight!"

Jacob snapped to attention like a recruit, but couldn't help wobbling back and forth.

"Where do you live?"

"Well...I just got into town and I don't have a place to stay yet, sir."

"I've got a place I can put you up for a few nights. It's called jail."

"No thank you, sir. I'm here to visit with my sons."

"Then what are you doing sleeping on my sidewalk?"

"Let me explain..."

"I don't need an explanation. Where do your sons live?"

Thinking for a moment, he said, "At 1641 Washington Street."

"Well, I suggest you go there to sleep it off."

"Can you please tell me how to get to Washington Street from here?" he asked the officer politely, afraid of angering him even more.

The officer gave Jacob directions and abruptly walked away. After taking a few steps, the policeman turned. With a stern glare toward Jacob, he shouted, "If I see you down here on my beat again sleeping on the sidewalk, you're going to jail. You got that?"

"Yes, sir."

Jacob headed in the opposite direction, already forgetting the directions the officer gave him. He hadn't really listened, still half asleep, and half in the bag from last night's diversion. As he walked, he began to cough. He coughed so hard that it made his head hurt. Jacob became sick to his stomach and ducked into an alley, where he leaned against the side of a building before sliding down into a sitting position. Putting his head in his hands, he began to vomit. He gagged and gagged, regurgitating the scotch he had consumed the night before. Blood began dripping from his mouth, blood he coughed up from deep within, an occurrence that happened lately with concerning frequency. It scared Jacob, causing him to wonder if he was sick, if he was dying.

Tears streamed from his eyes. He sat there, consumed by self-hatred, uttering aloud, "What a coward I have become. What a disappointment." Again, he began to reflect upon the days gone by. Over the last twenty-some years, he'd lived more in the past than he did in the present. The present was too painful, yet in many ways, so was the past.

He remembered the time he took Amanda to a cabin on a lake in the Illinois countryside. They took a canoe out onto the water. Like a new piece of shiny glass, the lake rested calmly against its surroundings under a cloudless blue sky. A crisp freshness permeated the air as the golden sunshine danced off Amanda's thick blond hair. As he rowed, Jacob couldn't take his eyes off her. She lay in the front of the boat, her bare feet dangling over the side as she dragged her fingers gently through the water. Her legs were long and slender, delicately extending from her movie star figure. And the best part? She was even more beautiful on the inside. Her unselfish demeanor was endearing to everyone she met. She dipped her hand into the water and blissfully splashed Jacob.

"Hey! Knock it off," he said playfully.

"Why? Are you afraid of the water?" She laughed.

She splashed him again. To retaliate, Jacob skimmed the oars along the top of the lake, spilling water into the front of the boat. Amanda curled up into the fetal position.

"Who's afraid of the water now?" He laughed.

"Stop it!" she squealed. "That's not fair!"

They began laughing as each of them splashed water onto the other. Suddenly, they stopped and looked deep into each other's eyes. Their lips met in a long kiss. They held each other close, kissing and caressing in the warm summer sun. Their bodies entwined, they lay in each other's arms, enjoying the moment as the boat drifted aimlessly on the lake.

★ ★ ★

"Excuse me. Sir? Are you all right?"

Surprised, Jacob opened his eyes to catch the image of a man kneeling over him. He was a kind-looking gentleman, clean shaven and properly dressed. His black hair had flecks of gray, and he smelled of spice from his aftershave.

"Yeah, I'm okay."

Jacob attempted to stand, but he was as wobbly as an antique table, falling back down.

"You sure you're all right?"

"Yeah, I'll be okay. Just give me a minute."

The man helped Jacob to his feet.

"It looks to me like you're in pretty rough shape."

"What? Are you a doctor or something?" Jacob replied, his tone caustic.

"No. I'm not a doctor, I'm a pastor. But I can recognize a

man who's in rough shape when I see him. How long has it been since you've had a meal?"

Jacob paused to reflect for a moment.

"A few days."

"Why don't you come with me down to the Salvation Army kitchen?"

The pastor took hold of Jacob's arm and the two started walking. Jacob had his legs now.

"What's your name?" the pastor asked.

"Jacob. Jacob McCallum. What's yours?"

"Howard Angel."

"Oh, you're kidding me, for crying out loud. I've been rescued by an Angel."

"Believe me when I tell you I've heard that one before."

Both men laughed as they continued their walk to the mission.

★ ★ ★

The front door to the Salvation Army creaked open.

"Well, here we are."

Jacob stood in the doorway and sized up the place. The stark interior was less than inviting, but the tantalizing aroma of eggs frying offered up a welcoming environment. The delicious fragrance of country ham also lingered in the air.

"Are you hungry?"

"I'm starved."

"Well, let's fix that."

Howard led Jacob over to the buffet. He got them each a plate, handing one to Jacob.

"Help yourself."

Jacob didn't need any more encouragement. He piled his tin plate high with scrambled eggs and carved off a thick slab of ham. Balancing two biscuits on the top of his food, he made his way over to the coffee urn for a fresh cup of morning brew. Howard went over to the table and took a seat, waiting for him. As Jacob took his place next to Howard, his mouth watered as he anticipated devouring his meal. Just then, his empty stomach let out an embarrassing growl. Jacob dug his fork deep into the mound of scrambled eggs and shoveled it into his mouth.

"Excuse me, Jacob," Howard interrupted. "But around here, we thank the Lord for his blessings before we eat His food."

Jacob, cheeks bulging, paused. His face reddened uncomfortably in recognition of his thoughtless faux pas. He wasn't accustomed to eating at a table these days, much less saying grace before he ate. Many years had passed since his last prayer. He'd given up on that a long time ago. Neither his manners, nor his grace, were as they used to be. He bowed his head while Howard gave the blessing, then he wasted no time satisfying his hunger.

"So tell me a little about yourself, Jacob."

"What do you want to know?" he said, chewing.

"A lot, but let's start with where you are from."

"Right here in Chicago. But I've been away for a while."

"Away? Where?"

"Here, there, and everywhere."

"Do you have a family?"

"Well…" Jacob paused.

"Well?"

"Yes. I do have a family, but I haven't seen them in a long while."

"Really? Why?"

"It's a long story. Believe me, you don't want to sit here and have to listen to it."

"Sure I do, Jacob. That's my job. And you look like you could use a friend right about now."

"Let's just say that I haven't been the most ideal father over the years. My kids...I say 'kids,' but they're all grown up now, well...they hate me."

"They hate you? *Hate* is a pretty strong word, Jacob. And I can't see how any child could truly hate their father."

"Well, trust me, mine do."

"How many children do you have?"

"Three. Two sons and a daughter."

"Do they all live here in Chicago?"

"My two sons do. I'm here to try to find them. I don't even know if the address I have is a current one."

"What are their names?"

"Tom and Frankie."

"Where does your daughter live?"

"She lives in the East—Baltimore, I'm pretty sure."

"Why don't you tell me a little about your children?" Howard quizzed, trying to get to the root of Jacob's problem without appearing too meddlesome.

"That's just it. I don't really know all that much about them. I've been in and out of their lives over the years— mostly out."

"Tell me what you do know, my friend."

"Do you have a smoke?"

"No," Howard said, laughing. "I don't smoke. And neither should you."

"Well, Emma, my daughter, is the oldest. Let's see, she'd be about, ah...thirty-one...maybe thirty-two. She's married, but I've never met her husband."

"Does she have any children?"

"Yeah. She has two—well, just a daughter now. Her son died when he was just a baby. I haven't seen or heard from Emma in six, maybe seven, years. I hardly remember my granddaughter. Tom, he's my next oldest. He'd be about...oh...I guess twenty-nine, almost thirty, and Frankie is my youngest."

"How old is your youngest son?"

"Let's see, Frankie would be in his mid-twenties or so."

"And your wife?"

"Amanda?"

"Is that her name?"

"That *was* her name before..." Jacob paused suddenly.

"Before what?" Howard asked.

Jacob took a sip of coffee and looked away from the table. His eyes began to well. He grimaced hard, attempting, unsuccessfully, to choke back his tears.

"What is it, Jacob?"

Jacob sniffed, then wiped his eyes and nose with the sleeve of his shirt.

"I don't want to talk about my family anymore."

"I'm here to listen, not to judge you. And frankly, you don't have to tell me if you wish not to."

"I'd rather not talk about it."

"That's okay. You don't have to."

"Really, I *don't* want to talk about it."

"Well, sometimes it's better to air things out that are bothering us."

Jacob's face hardened as he became agitated. "I said I don't want to talk about it!"

"Okay. Okay, Jacob. Then we won't talk about it."

Silence ended their conversation as Jacob hurriedly finished his meal. He stared down at his plate without looking up, without talking. Howard noticed periodic tears in Jacob's eyes. He wanted to get to the source of Jacob's pain, but he knew this was not the time.

"I hate to act like a hog," Jacob said. "But I'm really hungry. Can I get a second helping?"

"Sure you can."

Howard welcomed the opportunity for the extra time to find out more about Jacob. And judging from Jacob's drawn appearance, he was obviously malnourished and could use the extra helping of food.

As Jacob went back to the serving table, Howard poured them each another cup of coffee and returned to their table, waiting for Jacob to join him again.

"This is good ham," Jacob said while chewing.

The wheels were churning in Howard's head. Although he was accustomed to counseling troubled men of the streets, it had been a while since he'd encountered someone as troubled as Jacob appeared. He knew the despair of loneliness and rejection. Years ago, he'd found himself in a similar situation. He sensed Jacob's pain and his need for help. But he also knew he must choose his questions carefully.

"Tell me about your sons here in Chicago. Are they in the military?"

"I know Tom's not. He has a gimpy leg. I'm not sure about Frankie. Like I said, I've been out of touch for a while."

"What happened to Tom's leg?"

"Hey, look. I just would prefer not to talk about my family, all right?" Jacob said as he rose from the table. "If it's all the same to you, I think I'll be going now. Thank you for your kindness."

"Where will you go?"

"Wherever."

"Sit down, Jacob. Rest for a while."

"Nah, I better get going. I have some important things to do. Thanks again for your generosity."

"You know you're always welcome here. We're here to serve mankind," Howard told him.

"I'll keep that in mind."

As Jacob turned to leave, his face turned white. His eyes rolled back in his head and he fainted. Howard tried to catch him, but missed and Jacob hit the floor.

"Jacob, are you okay? " Howard said as he leaned over him.

Jacob went out for a few seconds before gathering his faculties and attempting to stand.

"Stay down, Jacob."

"I'm okay."

"It's obvious that you're not."

"Naaaah. I'll be all right," he said stubbornly.

Jacob made another effort to stand, but as quickly as he rose, he fell back down on a chair.

"Why don't you spend some time here?"

"No. I need to get going. I came here to find my sons—to make good with them."

"Nothing could be more important than your well-being. I insist that you stay here, at least for a while."

Jacob refused Howard's hospitality. As he tried to get up, he became woozy again. He held on to the side of the table to steady himself. Feeling too weak to stand, Jacob sat back down and reluctantly accepted Howard's offer to stay.

"If you don't mind, I could use a place to sleep tonight."

"I think you've made a wise decision. There's an empty cot in the back. You should lie down for a while."

Howard guided Jacob, still wobbling, to the cot, where he collapsed.

"I'll get you a blanket."

By the time Howard returned, Jacob was sound asleep. Not to disturb him, Howard unfolded the blanket and gently placed it on Jacob's tired body.

Howard took an immediate liking to Jacob. Later that afternoon, he went to the chapel and prayed for him. Afterward, he took a seat on the bench near the altar. He couldn't stop thinking about Jacob and wondering what lay ahead for this distressed man. He wondered what troubled him so. *Why would he say his children hate him? Why had he become so agitated when I asked him questions about his wife and children?*

Jacob slept through the day and into the night. Just past two in the morning he suffered an unsettling nightmare. In his dream he kept reaching out for Amanda, but just as their hands met, she would slip away from him. He abruptly awakened, startled, his shirt soaked from night sweats. Shivering, he sat up on the cot and wrapped the blanket around his shoulders. He rocked back and forth while he wept. Every time he closed his eyes, he could see Tom's bloodied body and Frankie trying to reach for his mother. He remained awake until after 4 a.m. before making an effort to get out of bed and leave the mission.

Feeling confined, he sought the freedom he felt when out on the streets. Placing his feet on the floor, he attempted to stand. Still too weak and overcome by fever, he laid his head back down on the pillow. For several more hours he battled sleep, fearful he would return to his nightmare. Eventually, sleep overtook him.

★ ★ ★

With a cup of hot coffee in his hands, Howard bent over the cot where Jacob lay peacefully, and softly tapped him on the shoulder. Jacob's eyes opened slowly, his nose quick to capture the smell of the freshly brewed cup of Joe.

"Here you go, Jacob. I thought you might need this to make you feel a little better."

"Thank you."

Jacob thought for a brief second and said, "I'm sorry, but I have forgotten your name."

"That's okay. My name is Howard. Howard Angel."

"Oh, yeah. How in the world could I forget that?"

They both chuckled.

"Yesterday was a difficult day for you and I completely understand. What do you say we get you some breakfast in your belly? I'm sure that will help restore your strength."

"Sounds good to me."

The two of them walked to the dining hall, where a plate of pancakes awaited Jacob. Hungrily, he attacked the plate.

"Remember, the rule here, we say our blessings before we eat."

"Oh, that's right, I forgot."

"Forgetting my name is one thing, but forgetting to give praise is another," Howard said gently.

They bowed their heads and Howard said a brief prayer. During breakfast, Howard, again, brought up the subject of Jacob's family and what was troubling him so. His attempt at conversation was met with the same result as the day before. Howard let it pass without another question.

As soon as Jacob had taken his last bite, he stood up.

"Where's my coat and my backpack?" Jacob asked eagerly.

"Seriously, Jacob, why don't you consider staying here for a few more days until you get back on your feet?"

"I appreciate the offer, but I have to go."

"Please stay."

"It's very generous of you to offer, but I can't."

"If you insist on leaving, then take this." Howard took some money from his wallet and handed it to Jacob.

"I can't accept your money."

"Call it a loan. You can pay me back when your fortunes turn."

Jacob's face contorted in protest as he slightly shook his head "No."

"Take it, please."

Jacob's eyes locked on Howard, who nodded.

"All right, I'll take it, but only as a loan, not charity."

They stood, shook hands, and Jacob left the Salvation Army Mission, heading back out into the streets of Chicago.

Chapter Five

Jacob walked about aimlessly, trying to summon the courage to visit his sons. As he walked, he thought about what he might say to Tom when he saw him, and what he would say to Frankie. What could he say? How could he make it all better with mere words? He envisioned the meeting and hoped it wouldn't turn out like his previous meetings had, with him and Tom arguing. The last time they saw each other, Frankie begged Jacob not to leave, but Tom felt much different. So Jacob, as he'd done many times in the past, left once again.

Jacob got off the streetcar at the corner of Wabash and Washington and walked up Washington Street to the row house bearing Tom's last known address. Stopping in front of 1641, he attempted to summon the grit to knock on the door, but before he did, he drifted back to a distant time, a time when he held Tom, his firstborn son, in his arms.

"Isn't he handsome?" Amanda said as she put her arms around Jacob and the infant son he held. Glancing up at Jacob, she smiled. "Just like his papa."

Jacob leaned in and gently kissed his wife on the lips. "I think he got his looks from his mom, not his pop."

Emma, a little more than two, toddled over and grabbed her father's leg. Jacob handed the infant off to Amanda, leaned over, and lifted Emma into his arms. "Speaking of beautiful, here's my little Emma," Jacob said with pride. He playfully held her over his head and blew air onto her bare stomach with his lips, making flatulent sounds, which always made Emma laugh.

"Jacob!" Amanda laughed.

"Oh, she likes it." He held her up and did it again, then held her close to his chest. She smelled so good. Jacob loved the scent of a freshly bathed baby.

The front door of 1641 Washington Street opened and a woman emerged. It wasn't Betty, Tom's wife, and it wasn't anyone Jacob recognized. She stared at him curiously as she walked by. Jacob let her pass, and then he said, "Excuse me, ma'am?"

She turned to him, a bit put off by his unkempt and soiled appearance.

"Are you talking to me?"

"Yes, ma'am," Jacob replied. "Do you live here?"

"I don't mean to be rude, but why is that a concern of yours?"

"Let me explain. My son, Thomas McCallum, and his family…this is the address I have for them. I have come a long way to visit."

"Well…yes, I do live here. But there's no Thomas McCallum in the residence. I've lived here for more than a year now."

Slipping his hands into his coat pockets, Jacob turned and slowly began walking away, gazing at the ground.

"Wait a minute, sir!" the woman said. Jacob turned around

hopefully. "There was a young man with his family who lived here before I moved in. I don't know where he moved to, but Mr. Schmidt may know."

"Mr. Schmidt?"

"Oh, he's the landlord. He may have your son's forwarding address."

"Where can I find this Mr. Schmidt?"

"He lives in the house on the corner," the woman said, pointing to a brick home up the street.

"Thanks. I'll give him a try."

"Good luck," the woman said as she turned and walked up the sidewalk.

Jacob stood there for another moment, thinking. *I'm so out of touch with my children that I don't even know where they live.* Redirecting his attention up the street to the house the woman had pointed out to him, he said aloud, "I guess I'll go have a talk with this Mr. Schmidt."

He proceeded up the hill, hopeful the man had a record of Tom's new address. Jacob walked up the front steps and onto the porch. Stopping at the wooden door with a large glass oval in the center, he knocked timidly—waiting for a moment before knocking again...this time louder. There was no answer. He walked across the front porch and peeked into the window to see if there was anyone home. There wasn't. Taking a seat on the front steps, he thought, *I'll just wait here for a while.* He watched as the wind raked the leaves from the tall oak tree in the tiny front yard. After sitting there for more than an hour, he decided to call it a day.

* * *

The moon rose over the Chicago skyline. Jacob, dejected by the day's events, found his way back to Kelly's Bar. He walked in the front door and found the joint filled with people—a rowdy crowd. Finding no seat at the bar, Jacob fetched a chair near the pool table, where two grizzly men were shooting a game of pool and drinking heavily. A wad of dollar bills lay on the corner of the table, waiting for the winner to grab. Curious, he observed them for a while. By habit, he fumbled through his pockets looking for a smoke. His search, as usual, was unsuccessful. Old habits die hard. He scanned the floor and spotted a cigarette butt that still had some life left in it. As he leaned over to snatch it, one of the inebriated fellows playing pool stumbled over Jacob's arm and fell to the floor. The place got real quiet.

"Hey! What's the idea of tripping me?"

As Jacob looked up, the burly man lifted himself off the floor, his unshaven face red with anger. The guy dusted off his pants with an ample set of hands, and then charged toward Jacob like a raging bull, grabbing him by the shirt, ripping it as he lifted him off the ground. The unruly crowd reacted with excitement.

"What's the idea, bub? What do ya got to say for yourself?"

Jacob said nothing so the brute shoved him to the floor.

"Get up! Get up and fight like a man!"

Someone in the crowd screamed, "Yeah!" Then everybody started shouting, trying to spur the big guy and Jacob into a fight. Jacob knew better. He got up, but not to fight. He turned to walk away and the man shoved him again.

"You're yella!" the man hollered.

The crowd began jeering Jacob.

"Look, I don't want any trouble."

"Then don't go around tripping people."

"I didn't mean to trip you."

The man charged Jacob again, this time with his fists clenched in a fighting posture. The crowd cheered its approval. Suddenly, an even larger man grabbed Jacob's aggressor from behind.

"Hold your water, Henry."

It was the bartender—thankfully not the one whom Jacob had the pleasure of meeting the previous morning.

"Well, he started it! He tripped me!" the man bellowed.

"I saw the whole thing, Henry. He was reaching for something on the floor and you stumbled over his arm. If you weren't so darn drunk, you wouldn't have fallen down."

"Let go of me!"

"I'll let go of you when you settle down, and not a minute before."

"All right. All right! I'm fine now!" the man snapped angrily.

"Okay. I'm going to let go of you and here's what you're going to do. You're going to get your hat and coat, and you're going to leave for the night without saying another word to this gentleman. Right?"

"Gentleman? You call this bum a gentleman?"

There was a pause. The bartender, still grasping the man from behind in a bear hug, gave another squeeze and leaned back slightly, lifting Henry, causing his boots to hover about two inches off the floor.

"Right?" the bartender demanded, this time using more persuasion.

"All right."

The bartender released him and Henry swaggered out the door, mumbling under his breath.

"I'm sorry for the trouble," Jacob conceded. "But thank you. I think I was in for a hard whippin'."

"Oh, don't mind Henry. He can turn pretty nasty when he gets a snoot full, but he's not a bad fellow, really."

"Here," the bartender said, offering Jacob a cigarette. "This will be better than the one I saw you reaching for on the floor."

"Thanks."

"You look like you're a little down on your luck. Are you from around these parts?"

"Originally, but I've been on the road awhile."

"Family here?"

"Yes. I have two sons here in Chicago."

"Are you staying with them?"

"Well, hopefully I will be when I find them."

"Where are you staying in the meantime?"

"Actually, I just got into town and I don't have a place to stay."

"Tell you what," the bartender said with a smile. "You look like you could use a hand, and so could I. If you stay and help me clean up the place after we close, there's a cot in the storeroom you can sleep on for the night. You'll be locked in after I leave, but Carl, my partner, will let you out when he opens in the morning. You can tell him I said you could stay the night, and I'll leave him a note, as well."

"By the way, my name's Bill Austin," the bartender said, extending his hand to Jacob. "What's yours?"

"Jacob McCallum," Jacob reciprocated, noticing the hugeness of the man's hand as he shook it. It appeared more like a bear's paw than a hand as it clamped down on his like a vise.

"Thanks. I appreciate it," Jacob said.

"Here, you could probably use one of these, too," Bill said as he poured Jacob some whiskey into a glass.

"I sure could."

The two men talked for a while. As the place emptied out, Jacob began putting the chairs upon the tables and swept the floor. After he helped Bill wash the last of the glasses, the place looked pretty tidy.

"Well...I guess I'll be leaving now. The cot's in the storeroom behind the bar. Carl will be in around eight o'clock in the morning to open up. He can let you out. Good luck finding your sons."

"Hey, I appreciate all your help," Jacob said.

"Don't mention it."

Bill turned out the lights as he left, leaving just a dim lamp on over the bar. Jacob heard him lock the door from the outside, and then shake the lock, making certain it was latched. Bill had left an open pack of cigarettes on the bar. Jacob assumed they were for him. He retrieved an ashtray, turned off the light, and retreated to the storeroom, where he reclined on the cot, lighting his cigarette. The cot felt good against his aching back. He set the ashtray on his chest and drew deeply on his smoke. The red glow turned amber, lighting his surroundings. He inhaled, filling his lungs to capacity. Holding his breath for an instant, he exhaled fully, expelling all the smoke from his lungs. Emotionally and physically drained, Jacob let his mind drift as he took an accounting of his life. How could he have let his life slip away, a life that by almost every measure had been perfect? He reflected upon his relationship with Amanda, and how, from the first day he laid eyes on her, he knew she would be his wife. Initially, she wasn't quite as convinced. But after months of Jacob's relentlessness, she warmed to his brash ways, and once she did, you couldn't pry her and Jacob apart. When times were good, they shared an especially deep love—until Jacob destroyed it, that is.

Jacob extinguished his cigarette, setting the ashtray on the floor. He sprawled on his back, raising his arms above his head, cradling it in his interlocked fingers. By now, his eyes had become accustomed to the darkness. A faint light from the street crept into the room through a small window, allowing him to see the slight shadows. He looked around the dirty room, which, with the exception of a few cleaning supplies and boxes, was virtually empty. Jacob remembered a time when he wouldn't have been caught dead even sipping a drink in a place like this, let alone sleeping on a cot in the storeroom because he had nowhere else to stay. Jacob's former life took him to the finest hotels in New York, San Francisco, New Orleans, and other cities from coast to coast. As he lay there, his eyes became heavy with sleep and he let his mind drift to a more peaceful place.

It was 1905. Jacob and Nick had just taken over a small manufacturing business that Nick's father had started about fourteen years before. The business manufactured brakes and other parts for the railroad industry. It was small, but provided a decent living for twenty-three people. Nick and Jacob started out working for Nick's father, forging steel. But when Nick's father became ill, Nick and Jacob hatched a plan to become equal partners and buy the business. They bought Nick's father out over time. Jacob and Nick set up a new corporation, J & N Manufacturing, of which each held fifty percent of the stock. They agreed that if either of them died, the surviving partner would purchase at least one additional percentage of the company's stock, making him the majority owner.

The young men approached their new venture with much vigor and enthusiasm. They were never satisfied, working long hours to manufacture better parts. Their efforts paid off as they developed a reputation for reliability and their business flourished.

One Sunday afternoon in June, Nick dragged Jacob to a family gathering to celebrate his Aunt Helen's birthday—a picnic in Nick's aunt and uncle's backyard. Jacob didn't really want to go, but went as a favor to Nick. On the way, Nick reassured him, "We'll just stay for a little while, and then we'll leave."

As they made their rounds greeting Nick's relatives, Jacob's eyes locked on to the most beautiful creature he'd ever seen.

"Who's that?" he enthusiastically asked Nick.

"Oh. That's my kid cousin, Amanda."

"She's no kid. She's beautiful. How old *is* she?"

"She's only seventeen, too young for you."

Seventeen, Jacob thought. *That's not too young.* Jacob was twenty-one at the time and hadn't dated much—being too busy with the business. He studied Amanda as she moved from person to person, her magnetic personality seeming to captivate all those to whom she spoke. She moved about so gracefully, making the sunny summer day even brighter for Jacob. Her blond hair glowed like a golden halo in the afternoon light.

"Nicky, how are you?" Amanda said as she rushed up to him. "I hear your business is doing great. We're all so proud of you."

Jacob stood by, jealous of all the attention being showered on Nick by the girl he was dying to meet. *Like Nick had done it all by himself*, Jacob thought. *How about introducing your business partner over here*, he said silently.

Amanda just kept talking away. She touched Nick on the arm

as she spoke. It was driving Jacob crazy. *Hey, Nick!* Jacob shouted in his mind. *How about introducing me! Surely he will,* Jacob reasoned.

Amanda rose onto her tiptoes, calling Jacob's attention to her long and slender legs as she kissed Nick on the cheek, then turned to walk away. *Hey, Nick! Over here! I can't believe he's going to let her walk away without introducing us.*

"Hey, Nick. Thanks a lot!" Jacob said after Amanda was gone.

"For what?"

"For nothing."

"What do you mean?"

"Thanks for introducing me to your cousin," Jacob said rhetorically.

"But...I didn't."

"That's my point."

"Oh, you wanted to meet her?"

"Now we're getting somewhere."

Nick grabbed Jacob by the arm and pulled him over to where Amanda stood in conversation with another guest.

"You don't have to be so obvious," Jacob said as he offered a bit of insincere resistance.

"You said you wanted to meet her, didn't you?"

"Yeah, but could we be a little more subtle?"

"Subtle?"

"Yeah!"

"Do you want to meet her or not?"

"Of course I do."

"Then come on!"

"Amanda!" Nick shouted, attracting everyone's attention. "There's someone here who wants to meet you."

Oh, what a great introduction, Jacob thought.

"This is my friend and business partner, Jacob McCallum."

"Hello, Jacob. It's a pleasure to meet you," Amanda said as she extended her hand. She favored Jacob with an endearing smile, her electric blue eyes staring straight into his.

Jacob awkwardly took her hand, which felt like a kidskin glove. He wasn't prepared and at a loss for words. He just stood there like an idiot, his heart pounding in his chest, unable to speak. *Say something, stupid!* his inner voice cried out. But his body wouldn't respond.

"Well...it was nice meeting you. Maybe I'll see you around sometime," Amanda said as she turned and walked away, a bit perplexed.

"You sure are smooth with the ladies," Nick joked. "I'll bet you made a memorable impression."

Jacob couldn't believe he'd fumbled the opportunity to meet the girl of his dreams. He just stood there, gawking at Amanda from afar.

"Are you ready to go?" Nick asked.

Jacob didn't even hear him.

Nick punched him on the arm. "Let's go, Romeo."

"Why don't we hang around for a little while longer," Jacob said, unable to peel his eyes off Amanda.

"You didn't even want to come here in the first place."

"I've changed my mind."

"Forget about it, Jacob. You blew it."

"What I wouldn't give for a second chance."

"Well, you're not going to get it this afternoon. Let's go."

Nick gave his Aunt Helen a good-bye kiss, wished her a happy birthday, and departed as promised with his friend.

Nick and Jacob walked several blocks to the station and caught the L train back into town, just a few miles away. All the while, Jacob couldn't stop thinking about Amanda, the most beautiful girl he ever met—or...sort of met...anyway.

* * *

Jacob obsessed over Amanda for weeks after their introduction. He kept prodding Nick to set them up with a date. Nick resisted the role of Cupid, however. Jacob would have gone calling on her himself, but after the fiasco at their initial meeting, he figured he needed all the help he could get.

One Monday at work, Nick and Jacob discussed what they'd done over the weekend. Nick described the delicious Sunday dinner he'd enjoyed at his Aunt Helen's. Jacob immediately began to cross-examine him about Amanda.

"What was she wearing? How did she look? Did she mention me?"

"Amanda. Amanda. Amanda. That's all you ever talk about. You only met her once. You didn't even speak to her. I doubt if she even remembers you after that great first impression you made."

"I know, but she's always on my mind. She's the most beautiful girl I've ever laid eyes on. You've got to arrange for me to meet her again."

"What if she already has a fellow?"

"Does she?" Jacob asked desperately.

"I don't know, but she might."

"I don't care. I really want to see her again."

"Well, I suppose if I want to get any work out of you, I better do as you ask. You've been moping around like a beaten puppy since you met her," Nick relented. "My aunt's back fence needs mending. She's always saying Uncle John keeps promising to fix it, but he never does. She mentioned it as I was leaving yesterday. Maybe next Saturday, you and I will drop by and fix it for her. That will be your excuse to see Amanda again."

"Thanks, Nick, I really appreciate it."

"But this time, practice your lines, will you?"

"That's real funny, Nicky boy."

The days of the week passed ever so slowly for Jacob as he anticipated another chance to meet Amanda. He couldn't believe he let Nick rope him into fixing a fence, though. But the opportunity to redeem himself in Amanda's presence seemed well worth it to him.

Finally, Saturday rolled around. Jacob and Nick caught the L and arrived at Nick's aunt and uncle's just after ten in the morning. Nick knocked on the door and his Uncle John answered.

"Nicky! What a surprise. Come on in."

"You remember Jacob, don't you?" Nick said, introducing his friend.

"Sure. You guys are getting quite a reputation around town. Real go-getters."

"Good to see you again, Mr. Lewis."

"Oh, you don't have to call me Mr. Lewis. You can call me John."

"Thank you, John," Jacob said respectfully.

"Who was at the door?" Nick's Aunt Helen asked her husband as she entered the room. "Nicky!" she said with surprise as she rounded the corner from the kitchen. "And you brought your friend Jacob."

"What brings you young men out this way, business?" John asked.

"No. Actually, we came out to fix the back fence."

The truth being there was a conspiracy afoot for Nick to introduce Jacob to Amanda...again.

"Yeah, I've been meaning to fix that fence for a couple of years now. I'll give you guys a hand."

"Oh, that's all right, Uncle John. We can manage. Besides, that's the least I can do to show my appreciation for the delicious meal Aunt Helen fed me last Sunday."

"That's mighty nice of you and Jacob," Helen said as she glared at her husband.

"Is Amanda home?" Nick asked his aunt.

"No, she spent the night with a girlfriend. I don't expect her home until late this evening. I believe she said something about going up to the lake with her friend's family. Did you need her for something, Nicky?"

"No, I just wanted to say hello."

"I'll give her your regards when she returns."

Well, that's just dandy, Jacob thought. *I came all the way out here to meet the girl of my dreams and she's not even here. Now I'm stuck fixing a fence on a beautiful Saturday! Why didn't Nick check to make sure she'd be here?*

"The tools are in the shed out back," John told them. "You guys sure you don't need an extra hand?"

"No, Uncle John, we can handle it, but thanks."

As they examined the fence, Jacob, with clear irritation in his voice, said, "Why didn't you make sure Amanda was going to be here? That's the whole point of this, isn't it?"

"Look, I didn't know. I just assumed she'd be here."

"Well, you obviously made the wrong assumption!"

The project wasn't as easy as Nick had anticipated. A number of the boards were rotten and needed to be replaced. The job ended up taking most of the day.

"Ouch! Dang it, Nick. Watch what you're doing!" Jacob shouted as he threw down the board he held and grabbed his left thumb, which throbbed with pain.

Nick had missed his mark with the hammer and slammed it down on Jacob's hand.

"Sorry, Jacob."

"Sorry? You're sorry? I'm the one who's sorry. Here I am wasting a perfectly good Saturday helping you fix a fence, with a smashed thumbnail, all so I could meet a girl—who's not even here!"

"Well, if you could have got your tongue dislodged from the roof of your mouth the first time you met her, you wouldn't be here now—would you? You're sorry, all right!"

They both started to laugh, Jacob forgetting momentarily about the pain coming from his aching thumb.

After completing the job to the satisfaction of Nick's Aunt Helen, she invited them to stay for supper. Before replying, Nick and Jacob looked at each other. Though grateful for the invitation and Nick's aunt's anxiousness to show her appreciation, Jacob considered all the other things he could be doing—especially in light of the day falling so short of his expectations.

Nick, sensing Jacob's reluctance to stay, spoke up. "Thank you very much, Aunt Helen, but we have to be going."

"I baked an apple pie," she said as an enticement.

Jacob gave Nick a look of certain death if he changed his mind.

"No, Aunt Helen. Thanks, but we'll be going."

"Thank you, boys, for fixing the fence," John said. "I was going to get to that next week."

Helen eyeballed her husband, smiled, and said, "Sure you were, dear."

"Not a problem, Uncle John," Nick said as he winked at his aunt. "We'll be going now, Aunt Helen." Nick kissed her on the forehead before leaving.

Jacob and Nick were about halfway down the block when Nick looked back and saw Amanda walking up to the front door.

"Oh no," he said as they continued to walk.

"What?"

"You're not going to like this."

"What?"

"I just saw Amanda go into the house."

"What?"

"I just saw..."

"I heard what you said. I just can't believe it. Of all the dumb luck! I came out here to get another chance to meet her. Instead, I end up spending the day with you fixing a fence, turn down a meal—and I'm starved, by the way...Amanda wasn't even home, then she shows up a minute after I leave...and all I have to show for it is a smashed thumb! You've got to do something, Nick."

"What do you want me to do?"

"Think of something!"

"Well...If you hadn't been in such a darn hurry to get out of there, we'd be eating supper right now, you could be gawking at Amanda, and I'd be about fifteen minutes away from enjoying some delicious apple pie."

"We have to go back and say we forgot something," Jacob conspired.

"But what?"

"You left your billfold out by the fence."

"No, I didn't."

Jacob swore at his friend. Then he said, "I know you didn't, but that will be our excuse to go back."

"You better get it right this time, Jacob, because I'm not going through this again just so you can meet Amanda. Now let's go!"

Nick knocked at the door. Amanda answered. She looked fantastic. The sight of her made Jacob's day worth reliving, except perhaps for the part about his throbbing thumb. She wore a dark blue dress with a flowered print that fit her frame snuggly, accentuating her slim figure.

"Nicky. What are you doing here?"

"It's a long story. Jacob and I were here earlier fixing your mom's fence and I think I left my billfold out in your backyard. I came back to get it. You remember Jacob, don't you? You met him at your mother's birthday party a few weeks ago."

Amanda looked at Jacob with uncertainty, then politely said, "Sure, I remember meeting him," though she didn't seem quite positive. "How are you doing, Jacob?"

"Fine," he replied.

"I'll let you two catch up on old times while I go get my billfold," Nick said with a touch of sarcasm.

Well…this was the moment Jacob had wished for. He felt a lump begin to swell in his throat. His mouth became dry. *Not again*, he thought.

Amanda broke the ice.

"Why don't you come in and sit for a while."

"Thank you. That would be nice."

They walked into the sitting room to join Nick's Uncle John and Aunt Helen.

"I thought you and Nicky left," John said.

Jacob explained why they came back.

"Did Nicky find it?" Helen asked.

"I don't know, he's in the backyard now looking for it," Jacob answered. He actually felt somewhat guilty telling the little white lie.

"How has your business been going?" Amanda asked.

"Great," replied Jacob. "We've been real lucky."

"Dad says it's more than luck. He says you and Nicky are going to be very successful one day."

"I sure hope he's right."

"Well, just remember good old Uncle John when it happens." John laughed.

"I found it," Nick said as he entered the room, holding up his billfold.

Jacob couldn't keep his eyes off Amanda. She caught him staring at her several times. His eyes would dart away when she looked back.

Amanda glanced down and noticed Jacob's mangled thumbnail. "What did you do to your thumb?"

"Nick hit the wrong nail," he said, holding up his swollen digit for everyone to see. He glanced over at Nick as everyone laughed.

"Believe me. He deserved it," Nick joked.

"That looks sore," Amanda said sympathetically.

"Yeah, it hurts a little bit," Jacob retorted in a manly tone to ensure that Amanda didn't perceive him as a wimp.

Amanda stood and walked over to Jacob. His eyes followed her every move as he scanned her body, beginning with her feet, up her long legs and torso, and they came to rest as he gazed up at her eyes.

"Why don't you come out in the kitchen and let me clean that up and put a bandage on it for you."

Jacob immediately jumped to his feet and followed her into the kitchen. She drew some water and, with a clean cloth, gently scrubbed the dried blood from his thumb. They stood close, Amanda bending over slightly in front of Jacob to get a good view of his injury. Jacob's eyes were active as they took in Amanda's beauty. He couldn't help himself. He leaned in slightly to get even closer. He could smell the sweet scent of her hair, closing his eyes to heighten his senses.

"Ouch!" Jacob shouted suddenly. Instantaneously, his ecstasy turned to pain and his eyes opened wide. "What are you doing?"

Amanda stood upright and proudly displayed the object of her surgery—his thumbnail.

"It was just hanging on there by a thread. I had to pull it off so it would heal properly," she said.

She gently wrapped his thumb with a clean bandage and they returned to the sitting room, rejoining Nick and Amanda's folks. Nick and Jacob ended up staying for supper that night, which made them both happy. Nick got his slice of apple pie. Jacob got to spend time with Amanda.

By midweek, Jacob's head still remained in the clouds over Amanda. He found it hard to concentrate—difficult to get any work done. Nick's patience with his partner wore thin.

"Come on, Jacob. You haven't been good for anything all

week. Don't make me regret introducing you to Amanda. I need you here."

"I'm sorry, Nick. I just can't stop thinking about her."

"You've got it bad. Why don't you do something about it?"

"Like what?"

"Ask her for a date. Take her candy, flowers, I don't know. Just do something so you're not so useless around here."

The truth was, Jacob longed to call on Amanda, but every time he got up the nerve, he got cold feet. That evening he bought some flowers and took the L out to Amanda's house. When he arrived, she was sitting on the swing that hung from the rafters above the front porch, her attention absorbed by a book. She hadn't even noticed Jacob as he walked up the sidewalk, bouquet in hand.

"Hello there, Amanda."

His words pierced the silence and frightened her, causing her to jump.

"Well, hello, Jacob. I didn't expect to see you so soon. How's the thumb?"

"It's great!" He held it up. "Practically brand new."

"But you've taken the bandage off. You shouldn't have."

"Oh, it's all right. You did such a good job patching it up that it's healing real good. Here, these are for you," he said, timidly handing her the flowers.

"They're beautiful, and they smell so lovely. But why are you bringing *me* flowers?"

"Because I wanted to, and to thank you for taking care of my thumb."

"Oh... That's sweet of you, and I appreciate it. But it wasn't really necessary."

"All right then, I'll take them back," he joked.

"Oh, no you won't!" Amanda said playfully. "It's not every day a girl gets flowers, you know."

If you were my girl, I'd bring you flowers every day, Jacob thought to himself.

Amanda moved over and made room for him on the swing, patting her hand on the cushion to invite him to sit next to her.

Jacob practically fell over himself at the suggestion. She lifted the bouquet to her face, taking in the pleasant aroma of the flowers once again. Looking over at him, she smiled and said, "Thank you, Jacob. That was very nice of you."

Jacob couldn't help blushing. They remained on the swing and talked for about an hour. Amanda quizzed him about the business, how he liked working with Nick, and she even asked questions about him, giving him the mistaken impression that she was interested. Jacob let Amanda do most of the talking. He loved listening to her voice and felt contented just being in her presence.

"I really must be going in."

"Yes. I need to be going also," he said, though truthfully, he would have stayed for several more hours if he could.

An awkward period of silence followed. Then, Jacob blurted out, "I'd really like to see you again."

"Sure, anytime," Amanda said, misinterpreting his intentions.

"I mean...well...what I mean is, I'm attracted to you and I would like to take you out on a date—to dinner or something," he said clumsily.

Amanda nervously inspected the flowers. Then, biting her upper lip, she peered back at Jacob. Mouth open, eyebrows raised, he anxiously anticipated her answer.

"I think I should tell you that I'm seeing someone."

"Is it serious?" he asked, bracing for the painful response.

"I wouldn't say we're going to get married or anything—not just yet anyway. But I have feelings for him and we've been seeing each other for a while."

Another uncomfortable pause punctuated the conversation. Jacob's face turned ash white. He felt queasy. Amanda's answer was absolutely deflating.

"What's his name?"

"Does that really matter?"

"Not really. But it would be nice to know the name of my competition."

"Competition?"

"You didn't think I was going to give up this easily, did you?"

She laughed. "Somehow, I didn't think you would. His name is Robert. But I wouldn't say you are his competition."

"By that, do you mean I'm not his competition, or he's not my competition?"

"Either way, this is *not* a competition."

"So what you're saying is there's still hope for me."

She shook her head and smiled. "Somehow, you impress me as a fellow that doesn't like to lose."

"I can only accept losing after I give my best. Could I just come over sometime and take you for a walk or something?"

"I'm not so sure that would be proper, since I *am* seeing Robert."

"Oh. So you aren't going to make this easy on me, are you?"

Amanda placed her hands over his. Looking up at him, she said, "Thank you for the wonderful evening and for the beautiful flowers. I'm sure we'll see each other again soon at a family gathering or something. That's if Nick brings you." She smiled in an ornery fashion.

"I'll make him bring me." Jacob laughed.

They hesitated, exchanging glances before saying their farewells. Jacob watched as Amanda opened the door and went inside. Then, he began his walk back to the train station. The evening, which had begun with so much promise, ended on a flat note—at least for Jacob.

J & N Manufacturing continued to flourish, as did the business reputation of the two young men who were behind it. Once they were content with the quality of their product and their manufacturing operation, Jacob and Nick hit the road, calling on the purchasing agents for the rail yards around Chicago, Detroit, and other major cities in the Midwest. Little by little over the next few years, their business grew even more. As the demand for their products increased, the entrepreneurs expanded their manufacturing facility. They also purchased land and buildings to expand further. The demand for their products became so high they could not seem to expand fast enough to keep pace.

* * *

Back at Kelly's Bar, Jacob dreamed randomly. In one of his dreams, he stood at the jewelry counter of a fine department store in downtown Chicago, an array of rings, bracelets, necklaces, and the like displayed before him. He spent almost a half hour studying the exhibit.

"I'll take that one," he told the woman behind the counter.

"Oh my. That's an excellent choice. Who's the lucky lady?"

"My wife, Amanda. It's her birthday."

"This must be a very special birthday."

"All of her birthdays are special. In fact, every day I spend with her is special."

What a catch, the woman thought.

They dined at an exquisite restaurant. Jacob couldn't wait to give the gift to Amanda. He'd planned to wait until after dinner, but his enthusiasm got the best of him. Just after ordering their entrées, Jacob told Amanda that he had a birthday surprise for her.

"Close your eyes and don't open them 'til I tell you."

"What are you going to do?"

"Just trust me. Close your eyes."

Amanda obliged.

Jacob pulled a stunning diamond necklace from his suit pocket. Leaning in, he gently placed it around her neck. The stones sparkled in the candlelight.

"Okay. Now you can open your eyes."

"Oh, Jacob, it's beautiful."

She took her compact from her purse and admired the necklace in the mirror.

"Do you like it?"

The pleased expression on her face told the story.

"I love it! You're so thoughtful."

Amanda slanted her body toward Jacob and kissed him softly on the lips. "I love you, Jacob."

Chapter Six

A rat scurried across Jacob's chest, startling him awake, tearing him from his wonderful dream. The dream served as a stark contrast to his current whereabouts—on a cot in the storeroom of a waterfront bar.

He rubbed the sleep from his face and fumbled for a smoke. As he lay there, he tried to return to the pleasantness of his dream but the demons in his mind wouldn't let him. Instead, they took him to another place—to a dark place where he did not want to go.

"No!" Jacob screamed. "No! I'm sorry, Amanda. I'm so sorry! Oh, Tommy—No! No!" he screamed again and began to wail. He cried, uncontrollably, for about an hour, cursing God and cursing himself. He was in hell. He got up and turned on the light, looking at the clock on the wall—4:30 a.m.

The place was closing in on him and he wanted to leave. He ran to the door, forgetting it was locked from the outside. He was a prisoner until the morning person came to open up at eight—just him and his demons.

His thoughts became bleak. He tried to go back in his mind where his pleasant dream had left off, but it was useless. He couldn't get away—or could he? Sure he could! Right there in front of him was the exit—the door to his escape. Why hadn't he seen it before? He could choose whichever door he wanted, vodka, scotch, rum—whatever. He chose scotch. That would be his way out. He walked behind the bar, pulled a bottle of scotch down from the shelf, and opened it. He started to pour it in a glass, then laughing angrily, he threw the glass against the wall, where it shattered into pieces. Jacob tilted his head back, taking a long swig of scotch straight from the bottle. He was on his way. Out of there!

Immersed in the agony of shame, self-pity, and regret, Jacob spent the next several hours chain-smoking and draining the contents from the fifth of booze that sat before him on the bar. He drank and wept, wept and drank, trying to forget all the tragedy in his life. He finally succeeded when his head hit the wooden counter on the bar. He passed out . . . escaping at last.

* * *

Whistling an old navy tune, Carl rattled the chain on the front door as he unlocked it. Upon entering, he immediately spotted the broken glass on the floor. His eyes shifted to Jacob—passed out, sitting on a bar stool, hunched over the bar—an empty bottle of scotch lay on its side next to his arm.

"What the . . ."

Carl pulled down a note that was tacked to the inside of the front door and read it.

Carl,

There is a gentleman sleeping on the cot in the store-room. He's just passing through and needed a place to stay. He helped me out last night cleaning and closing up so I let him stay for the night. Just thought I'd let you know.

Bill

Gentleman? This guy is a far cry from a gentleman, Carl thought.

"Hey. Hey! Wake up!" he yelled, shaking Jacob by the shoulders.

Jacob groaned, saying something completely inaudible.

"Wake up, you bum!" Carl bellowed, grabbing Jacob and pulling him to his feet.

Jacob staggered against the bar, barely able to stand on his own.

"What's the idea of helping yourself to a bottle of my best scotch? You got the money to pay for this?"

"Huh?" Jacob moaned, hardly able to open his eyes. Then he mumbled something else the bartender wasn't able to understand.

"Aren't you the guy that was in here a few mornings ago?"

"Yeah," Jacob slurred.

"Look at the mess you made, you old drunk. I suppose you don't have any money to pay for that scotch either—do you?"

Jacob was unable to carry on a conversation. He just leaned against the bar, swaying to and fro wearing an irritating grin on his face.

"Well, let's just see what you've got on you," the bartender said angrily as he ransacked Jacobs's pockets. He came up with two dimes, a nickel, three pennies, and a cigarette butt. "Yeah, that's what I thought."

The man gripped Jacob by the back of his collar and shoved him toward the door. Opening it, he tossed Jacob out onto the sidewalk as if emptying the trash. He returned in an instant and flung Jacob's ragged coat and knapsack out the door, hitting him in the face.

"Get out of here and don't you ever come back in this place again, or you'll be in for some real trouble!"

Now where had Jacob heard that before? He picked himself up, making several feeble attempts at putting his arms into the sleeves of his coat before staggering down the street away from Kelly's Bar. As he walked, he ricocheted off buildings and trees, bumped into several pedestrians, and was nearly run over as he staggered out into the street.

"Where do you think you're going—you old drunk," one man shouted out his car window over the sound of his horn. Several other drivers blew their horns at Jacob, as well, and a fellow even gave him the one-fingered salute, which Jacob happily returned—in a much more colorful fashion than he received.

He made his way several blocks from Kelly's before staggering to a stop. He sat down, leaning his back against the wall of Ben's Hardware, where he passed out again. As only Jacob's luck would have it, the same Chicago cop who, just the other day, had reprimanded him for sleeping on the sidewalk happened along.

Jacob lay facedown. The officer approached, tapping him on the back with his nightstick. "Move along, sir," the officer said.

Jacob didn't budge.

The officer rapped on Jacob's back a little harder with his stick. "I said move along!"

Jacob sat up, staggered to his feet, and the officer recognized him. "Oh, you again, eh?"

Jacob took one step, then stumbled to the ground.

"Okay, pal—let's go. I told you if I caught you sleeping on my beat again, I'd run you in. I guess you didn't believe me, did you? Well…I'm gonna make a believer out of you now."

The officer escorted Jacob to the nearest precinct and locked him in a cell until he sobered up. The last thing Jacob remembered as his head hit the pillow was how soft the jailhouse bunk felt. With a grin, he thought, *These accommodations ain't all that bad.* Then he passed out again.

★ ★ ★

Hearing a vaguely familiar voice approaching, Jacob began to awake. "Jacob. Jacob, wake up."

He squinted as he attempted to focus on the frame of a man standing over him. His head throbbed.

"It's me. Howard Angel."

"Where am I?"

"You're in jail."

"What are *you* doing in jail, Howard? Why'd they lock you up?"

"They didn't lock me up, Jacob. They called and said there was a lost soul down here sleeping one off…I had an idea it might be you. Come on. Sit up a bit."

When he did, the room began to spin; his hands trembled.

Howard helped him to his feet. They exited the police station and entered a cab Howard had kept waiting to take them back to the Salvation Army Mission. Once there, Howard fixed Jacob some hot coffee and a sandwich.

"Now, do you want to tell me what's eating at you?"

Jacob remained silent.

"Come on, Jacob. I want to help you, but first you have to help me by being honest."

"Don't bother wasting your time on me, Howard. My soul's not worth saving. I have been a sinner for many years now and my destiny awaits me in hell."

"Well, I don't quite see it that way and neither does God. You know Jesus died on the cross for our sins... and they can be forgiven if we only seek forgiveness."

"Just forget about me. There are others more worthy."

"You're the one I'm most concerned about at this moment, Jacob. Now, level with me. Please let me help."

"There are many things troubling me, least of which is the condition of my spiritual state."

"That should be number one on your list."

"Look, I *am* a lost soul. You can't help me. Don't waste your time."

Jacob's lips tightened. He squinted, and his face wrinkled in pain. He looked horrible, and he felt even worse.

"Why don't you get some sleep and think about what I said."

Howard walked Jacob back to his room.

"You can sleep in my room tonight. Tomorrow, we'll fix you a place to stay on here until you can get yourself straightened out."

Jacob's condition left him with no strength to argue. Slipping off his shoes, he collapsed on Howard's bed. Howard left quietly, easing the door closed behind him. Before passing out, Jacob surveyed the room, which appeared neat and clean, yet barren. The off-white paint that covered the brick walls was peeling. A lone portrait of Jesus hung on the wall. There was a tattered leather-bound Bible on a table next to the bed with several pieces of paper protruding at odd angles, marking pages within the book. Intrigued, he sat up and reached for the Bible, then hesitated. He touched it cautiously, as if it were hot and would burn his hands. Lifting it from the nightstand, he placed it on his lap. Marshalling the courage to open the book, he thumbed through its pages. It had been many years since he'd held a Bible in his hands. Its words seemed so foreign to him and far too difficult to comprehend. Frustrated, he closed the Bible and carefully placed it back on the table, rationalizing in a childlike manner that if he put it back in its original location, it would be as if he'd never picked it up in the first place. Reclining, he lifted his feet up back on the bed, reaching over to turn off the light before trying to fall asleep.

Exhausted, and feeling bad, he tossed and turned restlessly. Craving a drink and a cigarette—just a sip or two to calm his nerves—he began scheming about how to slake his thirst, taking his mind off his troubles just long enough to fall asleep. His dreams transported him back to his courtship with Amanda.

* * *

Another bouquet of flowers just arrived, the third of the week. Amanda fumbled for the envelope to see what was written inside. Jacob had a way with words, and reading his notes always excited her.

Amanda,

Your glowing skin and beautiful smile take my breath away.

Jacob

She held the note to her heart and smiled. *He is relentless*, she thought. *Flowers, candy, and all his surprise visits. Will he ever give up?* Her feelings were becoming confused. On the one hand, she had a relationship with Robert, but on the other...little by little, Jacob was chiseling away at her heart.

Jacob's endearing ways were making a favorable impression on Amanda, and she felt a strong physical attraction. If it wasn't for Robert, she would embrace a relationship with Jacob straightaway. But the history with her beau presented an obstacle for Jacob because she felt an obligation to Robert. What troubled her most? It was a feeling of obligation more than anything else.

The flowers and candy from Jacob kept coming, as did many declined invitations to *"Just take a walk or something."* But this didn't dissuade him. Every now and then, he showed up, unannounced, with flowers or a box of candy to spend a few minutes with Amanda on her front porch. His persistence once led to a very awkward occasion.

One evening, Jacob stepped onto Amanda's front porch. He extended his hand, the one not holding the flowers, of course. "You must be Robert. I've heard so much about you, and now I have the opportunity to make your acquaintance."

Robert didn't quite know what to think, but being polite, he confusingly offered his right hand to Jacob. Jacob latched on to it and gave Robert's hand a hard squeeze. With the other hand, he presented the bouquet of flowers to Amanda. Robert stared at Amanda with a stupefied expression. His face flushed and he sneered back at Jacob.

"Oh, this is Jacob, a friend and the business partner of my cousin, Nicky," she offered as an explanation.

Robert seemed less interested in Jacob's status and was clearly annoyed at the intrusion. He whisked Amanda away, saying they were late for the picture show. Jacob smiled to himself as he watched them walk, arm in arm, down the side-walk. Robert looked back over his shoulder to see what had become of Jacob. Jacob gave him a nod of approval...as if Robert needed it.

Jacob's persistence and unpredictable presence served as an irritation to Robert on more than one occasion and, at times, caused friction between Amanda and her suitor. That was just fine with Jacob. He'd much rather see friction between them than sparks.

Chapter Seven

As the months passed, Jacob continued his pursuit of Amanda. He began falling in love with her and sensed her feelings toward him were warming. She flirted with him frequently and paid him more attention. A mutual attraction became undoubtedly obvious as they spent more time together, taking walks, sitting on the front porch swing, talking and laughing for hours at a time. One starlit evening he heard her say what he wished she'd said months before: "Jacob, your persistence has finally worn me down."

"What is that supposed to mean?"

"I have feelings for you."

"Feelings?"

"Yes, feelings."

"What kind of feelings?"

"You know what I mean."

"No, really I don't. Please tell me."

Jacob knew exactly what she meant. But he wanted her to come right out and say it with certainty.

"You have won your little competition. You have won my heart."

Now she just needed to let Robert know, something she dreaded.

A broad, gratified smile grew on Jacob's face. "So it *was* a competition."

"Oh, Jacob!" She smiled.

She buried her right cheek in his chest and hugged him close. Jacob wrapped his arms around her and gave a gentle squeeze.

"I love you, Amanda."

"I love you, too."

They embraced each other tightly.

The next day, Robert came calling. An awkward and uncomfortable conversation followed.

"What's wrong, Amanda?"

"Nothing."

"Something's up. What is it?"

She thought for a moment, contemplating how to tell him about her change of heart.

"What is it?"

She took a deep breath. *Here goes*, she thought.

Nervously she said, "We've been dating for a while, and I know you want to become more serious about our relationship."

"Yeah? And...?"

"I don't know if I want to continue our romance."

"What?"

"I'm sure you've been able to discern our bond has been strained lately. Things just haven't been the same."

"Yes, I have."

"I'd like to take a break."

"A break, or are you trying to tell me more?"

Amanda paused, looking up at him.

"Well, what I'm trying to say is…I want to slow down a little."

"Slow down, or stop?"

"Truthfully, I think we should stop seeing each other."

Stunned, he spoke a little louder. "Does this have something to do with your friend Jacob?"

"Ah…you might say that."

"I *am* saying that! I knew that guy was going to be trouble."

"I'm sorry, Robert, but I would like to go out with him."

"My suspicion is you already have. Haven't you?"

"Let's not argue."

"I can't believe this."

"I'm so sorry. I don't want to hurt you."

"Well, how did you think I was going to feel? Did you actually think I was going to be happy to hear what you have to say?"

"No, but that is truly how I feel."

"What did I do wrong?"

"You didn't do anything. We have grown apart."

"That's bull. This guy Jacob…he's the reason."

"Not totally, but I'd be lying if I said he didn't have something to do with it."

"That's what I thought. Well, you'll have your wish. I'll leave you to your new romance. I hope you're satisfied!"

"I don't want it to end like this—arguing."

"Well, you're not going to get that wish! Good-bye."

Robert turned and left abruptly.

"But, Robert…"

"Have a nice life with your new beau. I'm done wasting my time with you."

She watched him until he turned the corner and disappeared from her sight.

* * *

Amanda's romance with Jacob took off like a shooting star. They shared a deep love, one that each of them cherished above anything else in their lives. They were together every day—inseparable. On a chilly October night, Jacob and Amanda were returning from an evening stroll. As they walked up the front porch steps of Amanda's parents' home, Jacob turned Amanda to face him. He embraced her, then looked into her eyes. They gazed at each other for an instant before their lips met in a passionate kiss. As their lips parted, Jacob whispered, "I love you, Amanda. I love you more than I could have ever imagined loving anyone."

Jacob gently pulled her down on the swing.

"Let's sit here for a while and talk," he said.

"Why don't we go inside and talk, Jacob? I'm cold."

Jacob draped his jacket around her shoulders.

"This is where it all began for me, Amanda. Right here on this swing, my whole life changed. I want to spend a few more minutes with you right here."

He knelt before her. Amanda looked down at him curiously, thinking she knew what might be coming next. Her lips quivered slightly from the chill of the autumn night's air. Jacob held her hand and gazed into her eyes. Leaning forward, he kissed the back of her left hand before gently sliding a sparkling diamond ring on her finger.

"I want to spend the rest of my life with you. Will you marry me?"

Her lips quivered even more now, and it wasn't because of the cold. She fought back tears. Tears of joy. She surrendered to her emotions as tears rolled down her cheeks.

"Oh, Jacob. Yes, of course I'll marry you. You are the love of my life!"

She pulled him to her and they embraced as she wept with happiness. Amanda thought for a moment, then pushed Jacob's head back suddenly.

"But what will Papa say?"

"Don't worry. I've already discussed it with him, and your mother. They both think it's a fantastic idea."

Jacob and Amanda were married that December in a stunning candlelight ceremony. They honeymooned in the warmth of the Florida sun and began what would be, for a time at least, a wonderful life together.

★ ★ ★

Jacob awoke the next morning. As he walked out to the dining hall of the Salvation Army Mission, he saw Howard approaching.

"Sleep good?"

"Sure did."

"Care for a cup of coffee?"

"That sounds like a wonderful idea."

"Sit down at the table and I'll fetch us some."

Jacob found an empty table and waited for Howard to return.

"How's your head this morning?" Howard asked.

"Not too bad, actually. I had a good night's sleep, and a wonderful dream."

"Oh, yeah? What did you dream about?"

"A better time in my life."

"And?"

"I was dreaming about the days with my wife, Amanda. Those were such fabulous times."

"Tell me about it, Jacob."

"Nah. I keep my memories to myself, both good and bad."

"Jacob, pardon me for prying, but you need to come clean. It will do your soul good."

"My soul? I don't even know if I have a soul. I'm more of a heel," he said.

"Come on, Jacob, I want to help you get right with yourself, and your family. You can't keep this bottled up inside you or you'll be destroyed by it."

Jacob shifted in his chair, not wanting to reveal more, but he realized it would be helpful to confide in his new friend. He thought about his previous discussions with Howard, and his repeated offers to help Jacob overcome his heartache. He'd spent the last twenty years letting his past eat away at him, keeping his anguish to himself. He knew it would do him good to vent about his past. Keeping it to himself hadn't been working too well for him anyhow.

"You know, Howard, money and power often have ways of clouding one's judgment and corrupting one's values. I'm no exception. There was a time, many years ago, when I was a wealthy man. I had it all, a successful business, a dedicated friend and business partner, a beautiful wife, and absolutely wonderful children. My business partner, Nick, and I built a booming business from practically nothing."

Jacob told him about how his business had thrived, and about the many accolades he received for his hard work, honesty, and success...then how it all got away from him.

"What happened to your business?"

"It's very long and complicated."

"I'll listen as long as it takes."

Jacob's thoughts turned to the past. How, at the pinnacle of his life, he and Nick were on top of the world. Their business became immensely successful as the orders kept rolling in. They were at full capacity. Jacob traveled extensively, meeting and entertaining customers. He and Amanda were now living in a luxurious home with all the trappings of success.

"We had a great thing going, Amanda and I. We were deeply in love. As we had our children, our love for one another grew immensely. Life couldn't possibly have been any better."

"What happened?"

"The pressures of the business were tough. I had trouble handling it...all the success. I was traveling all the time. Alone on the road, I began drinking to pass the hours. That led to a lot of other unhealthy things. My drinking caused problems with Amanda. She was dead set against it, but it got so I couldn't stop."

"Did you try to get help?"

"No, I was too stubborn. Figured I could handle it myself—but I couldn't."

Jacob explained that his drinking kept getting worse. This

further troubled Amanda, who constantly complained about his extensive use of alcohol. It didn't help that Amanda's moral convictions were against such a thing, and prohibition made drinking a criminal offense. This made the situation, from Amanda's perspective, even more troublesome. His lack of regard for the law infuriated her. Though alcohol was tough to come by, a man of Jacob's means could readily find a source. Even while at home and not traveling, he spent much of his time at the office, or in speakeasies, where booze and women were in sufficient quantity. After a few years of the affluent lifestyle, Jacob and Amanda's marriage began to fracture.

"Where are you going tonight?" Amanda demanded one night.

"I'm going to the office, then I might stop by the club for a drink."

"We need to talk! If you don't stop drinking, I'm taking the children to my parents' and we'll stay there until you grow up and stop this nonsense."

"You've been saying that for months. If that's what you want to do, just do it and stop threatening me."

The truth? Jacob wasn't intending to go to the office that evening. He spent less and less time there and more time hanging around with the questionable characters in his favorite watering hole. His habit of drinking became more prevalent as he depended upon alcohol to get through each day.

Jacob went to the door of the speakeasy and gave the code name to enter. As the door swung open, he was greeted by Alfonzo Romano, one of Jacob's acquaintances he hung out with at the bar.

After a few minutes of conversation, a seedy character

approached Alfonzo. He was impressively dressed and possessed an intimidating presence. There was something alluring about the man, though. Jacob couldn't quite put his finger on it, but he found him intriguing.

"How are you doing, Al?"

"I'm doing great. I'd like to introduce you to a friend of mine. This is Jacob McCallum."

"Pleased to meet you. I'm Carmen Ricci."

"How do you know my friend Al?"

Jacob recognized the name. Carmen Ricci was a colorful character known around Chicago as a wheeler dealer of questionable sorts.

"Jacob is one of the owners of J & N Manufacturing," Al said.

"Oh, yes. I've heard of you. You're quite the man about town."

"Thank you."

"Your operation has been very good to you."

"Yeah, we've been fortunate."

"Why don't you gentlemen join me for the card game in the back room? I'll introduce Jacob here to some of the guys."

Jacob joined Alfonzo and Carmen in the back room. They made their way through the dense cigar smoke before coming to the poker table.

"Next hand, deal us in," Carmen commanded. Turning to an attractive cocktail waitress, he said, "How about a round for the boys...It's on me."

"Okay, sir, I'll be right back with your drinks."

As the three took their places at the table, Carmen introduced Jacob to his pals, all business associates. Several of them were chomping on large stogies. All the men at the table looked dubious. After lighting his stogie, a large fellow, with a noticeably pockmarked face, dealt the hand.

Just after midnight, a cop came into the back room. At first, Jacob thought it might be a raid. He quickly stood and bolted for the back door.

"Hold on there, Jacob." Carmen laughed. "This is Sam, a good friend of ours."

Everyone at the table got a big chuckle out of Jacob's reaction, especially Sam.

"You here to do business?" Carmen asked.

Sam nodded.

Carmen and Sam went behind the bar, where Carmen counted out some money and slipped it to the officer. The guys at the table stopped playing cards for a moment. The large man who dealt the cards blew his cigar smoke across the table at Jacob, giving him a menacing look.

Carmen returned. "That oughta take care of him for a while."

Everyone laughed, except Jacob.

Jacob remained there until early morning. Upon returning home, Amanda met him at the door. She'd waited up for him, her eyes tearstained and her face red with outrage.

"Where have you been? You don't have any respect for me at all, do you?"

Jacob staggered past her and into their bedroom, not at all receptive to Amanda's objections. He was close to passing out, and the last thing he wanted to do was argue. As he lifted his leg out of his trousers, he stumbled onto the bed. Amanda, clearly irritated, went to the living room sofa to sleep.

Jacob showed up for work more than two hours late, missing an important meeting with a potential new customer. Nick was outraged. "You're becoming totally unreliable. What's your problem?"

"I don't have a problem. You're the one with a problem...an attitude problem. Remember, I own half of the business, and because of me, this business has grown to be what it is today."

"You *have* been responsible for much of our growth, but you haven't done anything in the past few months that has amounted to a hill of beans. I'll tell you what your problem is, Jacob...the bottle. You can't seem to keep your snoot out of it!"

"Why don't you keep your nose out of my business and stop worrying about my snoot in the bottle, as you put it? I'm tired of people criticizing me for having a few drinks now and then."

"Now and then? You have got to be kidding me! You come in here hungover about every day. And when you're out on the road, you are constantly standing up customers and embarrassing me and the business."

"Embarrassing you? How dare you say that!"

"It's true. So I *will* say it!"

"Screw you. I'm out of here!"

Jacob abruptly left, slamming the door behind him. He went straight home to get some shut-eye. When he arrived, Amanda and the children were nowhere to be found, only a note.

Jacob,

I have been telling you for months that I am sick and tired of your drinking and irresponsible behavior. I am at my parents' house and I'll be staying here for a while.

Amanda

She finally did what she'd been threatening to do for months, and Jacob wasn't happy about it. He balled up the note in his hand and chucked it across the room. Immediately, he went to the liquor cabinet and poured himself a tall drink before taking a seat on the sofa. After sitting there for a moment, he retrieved the ball of paper off the floor and reread the note, feeling a bit ashamed. But after a few more drinks, he rationalized that he didn't really care. He took another hit of whiskey and threw the note into the trashcan.

"At least I don't have to hear her nagging me anymore."

To fill the void Amanda had left in his life, Jacob spent more and more time at the speakeasy with his new friends. One night, Al came over to Carmen while he conversed with Jacob.

"Carmen, I need to speak with you for a minute."

"I'll be right there."

Carmen gestured to Jacob that he'd be right back.

Carmen and Al walked away from the bar. Jacob overheard part of the conversation.

"They arrested him?"

"I thought we took care of Sam so this wouldn't be a problem."

Jacob remembered Carmen paying the policeman. The conversation confirmed his suspicions. It became abundantly clear that Carmen, Al, and the boys were involved in some shady business. He wasn't surprised. Jacob found their lifestyle oddly attractive. They were movers and shakers...always nailing down incredible business deals. Now he understood why. Though he was somewhat frightened, it all seemed mysterious yet captivating. The guys were flashy, well dressed, and liked a good time, unlike Nick, who by comparison, Jacob found boring. Besides, Nick was becoming too conservative with the business, always playing it safe. These guys were raking in the dough with their businesses and Jacob wanted to be a part of it.

Alfonzo and Carmen asserted a strong influence over him. Jacob's judgment became clouded by his constant drinking and womanizing. When approached to join them in a few business ventures, Jacob was more than willing. He got in deep...way over his head. These business ventures were not on the up-and-up. His uncharacteristic behavior was an obstacle to reconciliation with Amanda, as she remained at her parents' home...unwilling to return to live with Jacob. She found his new lifestyle repugnant.

J & N Manufacturing suffered from Jacob's frequent absence. At the end of his patience, Nick confronted Jacob. As Jacob became more profoundly involved with his new friends, he discovered they were involved with the mob and were swindling many unsuspecting souls out of their businesses. At first, he was alarmed. But it began to feel exhilarating. The crew became involved in a number of other illegal activities to which Jacob was an accomplice. His life quickly transformed from one of power, privilege, and respect to one of chaos and darkness.

★ ★ ★

"Well, Howard, there you have it—the story of my life—part of it anyway. What I told you is almost innocent compared to what happened next."

"Tell me more, Jacob." Howard was engrossed in the story.

Clearly troubled, Jacob looked away from the table, unable to make eye contact with Howard, tears welling up in his eyes.

He called out to one of the other residents of the mission, who had just lit a cigarette at an adjacent table.

"Could I trouble you for one of those?"

The man walked over to their table.

"Sure. Here, take two."

"Thanks, Will," Howard said.

"Yeah, thanks," Jacob echoed.

The man noticed the tears in Jacob's eyes, but didn't want to get involved in someone else's problems, having plenty of his own. He offered Jacob a light and walked back to his table. Jacob turned his attention back to Howard, who watched as a tear rolled down Jacob's cheek.

"There is much more troubling you."

Jacob took a deep drag on his cigarette and unconsciously blew the smoke across the table, causing Howard to cough.

"Sorry."

"Is that your answer to telling me the rest of your story?"

"You might say that. I just prefer not talking about the rest."

Since Jacob had agreed to stay at the mission for a while, Howard assumed there would be plenty of other opportunities to broach the subject again. He dropped the issue, though deeply troubled by what he'd just learned.

Chapter Eight

Over the next few weeks Howard worked with Jacob on changing his ways, to rebuilding his acceptance of faith and the prospect of forgiveness from his children. He continued his attempts to get to the root cause of Jacob's misery and more details about his children and his marriage, but Jacob remained resistant to offer more details.

One day, while having their morning coffee, Jacob seemed particularly preoccupied. Howard got the strong notion that there was something important Jacob needed to say.

"Not very talkative this morning, Jacob."

"Yeah, I've been doing a lot of thinking about my life. Howard, I want to get my old life back, to stop drinking and make things right with my children, but I just feel so unworthy."

"You're not unworthy, Jacob. You're just unwilling. If you're interested, we're starting a group here called Alcoholics Anonymous."

"Alcoholics Anonymous? What's that?"

"It's a new concept to help people like you."

"People like me?"

"To stop drinking. It's a faith-based program and it's been pretty successful so far."

"Faith-based? I'm a little short on faith at this point in my life."

"That may be your biggest problem, Jacob. Your lack of faith, in God and in yourself, is an obstacle that you have put in your own way."

The truth was, Jacob had lost faith in God many years ago. And as far as faith in himself, that seemed out of the question. He knew no one else had faith in him, so why should he have faith in himself?

"Well...what do you say?"

Jacob glanced down at the table then looked Howard in the eye.

"I don't think I'm ready for that just yet."

Howard frowned somewhat, disappointedly shaking his head ever so slightly.

"You're a hard nut to crack, my friend."

"I guess you could say that. But faith is something I seem to shy away from. I'm just not there yet."

"Until you get there, Jacob, I'm afraid there isn't much I can do for you. Not much you can do for yourself, either."

"This is all too foreign to me. I think I'm just a lost cause."

Howard felt disheartened and was losing patience. He knew Jacob would not be able to reconcile with his children if he refused to take responsibility for his role in the family's disunity. He'd played a major part, and until he accepted his need for faith and forgiveness in a serious way, it would elude him. Frustrated, Howard got up from the table. Before departing, he said, "I've got to attend to some other problems. We'll leave yours for now, since you refuse to deal with them."

Surprised at Howard's abruptness, Jacob watched as his only friend walked away, thinking Howard showed signs of giving up on him, too. But he could only blame himself. Why was he so stubborn? His reluctance to tell Howard more stood in his way and he knew it. It seemed like the easiest answer was to drink himself into oblivion and delay the entire matter.

His thoughts were interrupted when Howard returned to the table with a mop and a bucket. Puzzled, Jacob's eyebrows turned down.

"It's time you start earning your keep around here," Howard said as he held out the cleaning tools for Jacob. "The floor needs mopping and the closet in my office needs a good cleaning. I hope you'll think about what I said while you work. There's an old saying: 'It is the working man who is the happy man. It is the idle man who is the miserable man.' Now let's get to work," he said kindly.

Jacob wasn't amused. Standing, he grabbed the bucket and mop, a grumpy scowl on his face. The notion flashed through Jacob's mind to leave the mission and go back out on the streets to be on his own. But he liked Howard and knew the key to his redemption was within his grasp. At the moment, however, he was unable, or just unwilling, to open his heart.

As Jacob worked, his thoughts returned to the reason he came to Chicago. He was anxious to talk to Tom and Frankie, but he succumbed to his fears...to the certain rejection that he knew awaited him when he knocked on Tom's door. He couldn't bear the thought, but he knew he needed to confront it—just not yet.

* * *

Howard and Jacob continued to spend a lot of time together, which was good for Jacob. Howard's influence weighed heavily on him. They spent hours discussing the value and powers of faith and forgiveness and all the things Jacob needed to do in order to facilitate them. They even prayed together, something Jacob initially fought before giving in, before realizing the truth in his friend's insistence. Howard's tenacity began to wear Jacob down, and little by little he opened up more about what was troubling him so.

Truly evolving, Jacob did his best to quit smoking and drinking and to accept what he needed to change. He even caved in to the idea of joining Alcoholics Anonymous and enjoyed participating with the group at the mission. He did slip up over and over again. Even so, Howard refused to give up on him. It had been three weeks now since Jacob had had a cigarette, and even longer since he'd had a drink, doing so with the help of Howard and the support of some of the residents at the mission. Howard convinced the owner of a hardware store near the mission to give Jacob some part-time work. This did wonders for his self-esteem and afforded him some spending money. He continued his work at the mission, cleaning and helping Howard organize, as well.

While they were chatting one evening, the subject again turned to Jacob's past and to what was haunting him so. Forthcoming, yet apprehensive, Jacob divulged more about his past, something Howard welcomed as a payoff for all his patience and caring.

"Howard, I need to get some more things off my chest. Keeping them bottled up inside is killing me. I've done some terrible things in my life that I'm deeply ashamed of. Not just to my family, but to my best friend."

"I'm here for you, Jacob. Tell me all that you care to. Whatever it is you have to say, I can assure you it will remain between the two of us."

"I betrayed my best friend and my business partner."

Jacob closed his eyes and took Howard back with him into the past.

He resumed his story about the tremendous growth and success of J & N Manufacturing, and how Nick had become content with the way things were. But selfishly, Jacob wanted more. He wasn't satisfied with the slow but steady progress of the business. His greed left him with a yearning for more money, more power, and more excitement. His relationships with Amanda and Nick spiraled out of control to the point of destruction. As a result, he drank even more. He missed Amanda and his children, recognizing that his life was but an empty shell. Despite his involvement with his new friends, loneliness consumed his life. He quickly tired of coming home and not seeing his family. He begged Amanda many times to move back home, telling her he would stop drinking and change his ways. Repeatedly, she declined. It got so that Jacob stopped caring anymore. He stopped caring about everything.

A dissonance grew between Jacob and Nick. One morning when Jacob arrived at the office, late as usual, the friction between them came to a head.

"You've turned out to be a real slouch," Nick remarked.

"Why don't you mind your own business, Nick?"

"This *is* my business! And it is yours, too. I can't do this alone anymore. Either you start pulling your weight, or get out of here."

"Listen, Nick, I own fifty percent of this business, so don't tell me to get out."

"You're disgusting. I regret the day I went into business with you."

"Maybe I have my regrets, too."

"You do nothing but drink, hang around with your mobster friends, and carouse with loose women. You aren't worth a damn."

"Screw you."

"You've turned out to be a lousy husband and father, too! Just look at you. Amanda has told me how miserable you've made her life."

"Why don't you stay out of my marriage? It's not your concern."

"I regret the day I ever introduced you to Amanda. You have made her life hell. I oughta beat the crap out of you...you miserable louse."

Jacob got up in Nick's face.

"Go ahead if you think you're man enough."

"I'm much more of a man than you'll ever be!"

Jacob, his fists already clinched, struck Nick in the face, causing him to stumble backward.

"Get out of here before I make you regret what you just did!"

Jacob paused for a moment, cursed Nick, and then left.

One night during a card game at the speakeasy, Jacob was

approached by Alfonzo and Carmen, both sporting sinister looks.

"Let's go over to a table. There is something we want to discuss with you," Carmen suggested.

Jacob obliged. "What is it?"

Carmen began telling him about his dubious plan. "We have an interesting business proposition we'd like you to handle for us."

"What kind of a business proposition?"

"You've been complaining about your business partner holding the company back, and how much you dislike him, right?"

"Yeah, so what?"

"We have some investors who are interested in acquiring J & N Manufacturing. You could make a lot of money if the plan works. We'll buy your stock at a premium and there'll be a lucrative bonus in it for you when it's all settled. Believe me, there is plenty of money in this for all of us."

"What do you need from me?"

"Well...first of all, can we trust you?"

"That depends."

"On what?"

"On what you want me to do."

Carmen explained the details.

"Here's our plan. We'll create some shell companies which will pose as J & N Manufacturing vendors. We need you to alter the books and to begin to skim cash from the company to make it appear like it's losing money. We can cover it by billing J & N through our shell companies. We need you to pay the bogus invoices from the vendors. This will put the squeeze on your partner. When he is really hurting and realizes the business is failing, we'll come in and make an offer to buy the business at a low price and take control. We'll pay you an inflated price for your stock and then give you a part of the action. We'll make an immediate profit and expand the business like you have been wanting. We just need you to help set it up."

Stunned by Carmen's suggestion, Jacob never expected this.

Bowing his head, he stared down at his hands, which were clasped in front of him on the table before looking back at Carmen, staring him square in the face.

"I don't know. Sure there's hard feelings between Nick and me, but I don't know if I can do this."

"Why? This will give you what you want. Your partner will be out of the way and we can expand the business, making us all a fortune."

Jacob sat silent for a moment, then said, "I can't do it. I *do* have a conscience, you know."

"Don't let your high-brow ideals get in the way of a good business opportunity that's as easy as this. It'll be like taking candy from a baby."

"I don't know. It's really underhanded. You're asking me to betray my partner...someone I grew up with...someone who introduced me to my wife."

"You said he was a pain in your backside. What's the problem?"

"This is where I have to draw the line. Count me out."

"It's not like you haven't been involved in these kind of deals with us before. Remember the lumberyard deal? Then there was the two restaurants downtown."

"Yes, but nothing like this. I won't do it. I can't."

"What if your involvement in past deals would, let's say, accidentally come to light? What would that do to your reputation?"

"Are you threatening me with blackmail?"

"It's not a threat...just a suggestion. If your unscrupulous business dealings were somehow revealed...let's just say by some anonymous source...it could ruin your life."

"Well, your 'suggestion' hasn't changed my mind."

"Our investors want to move on this. It's very seldom that they don't get their way with things."

Alfonzo interjected, "Maybe you don't quite understand. Our investors want this done. Disappointing them could be bad for your health...and ours. It could even affect the health of your wife and children. These guys are ruthless."

Jacob got up, leaned across the table, red faced...the veins in his neck popping out. "You leave my family out of this. Do you hear me? I told you I won't do it...and that's it!"

Carmen grabbed Jacob's necktie and pulled his face toward him until they were nose to nose. "You *will* do this. You got that?" Carmen shoved Jacob back into his chair.

The ruckus caused a large gentleman to saunter over to the table from the bar. As Jacob attempted to get up, the oversized man put his hands on his shoulders and held him in his chair.

"Is there a problem here, sir?" the man asked. What he was really saying was, *Sit down, shut up, and don't you dare cause a problem.* "Mr. Ricci, would you like me and Tony to take Mr. McCallum here for a little ride to make him see things your way?"

"No, Mario, I believe Jacob is beginning to see things our way, so that won't be necessary."

"Okay, boss."

"Well, Jacob? Are you in?"

"I guess I don't have much of a choice. But I'm not in favor of doing this. I want you to know that."

"Like you said, you don't have much of a choice."

"Come on, fellas, can't you just let this one go?" Jacob pleaded.

"It is beyond our control," Carmen answered. "These guys don't take 'no' for an answer."

Jacob did as Carmen and Alfonzo demanded. He altered the books and falsified invoices. The plan seemed to be working. Profits at J & N Manufacturing plummeted. It appeared that the company was losing money. Nick, truly distressed and unable to grasp how this could be happening, was in disbelief. Jacob feigned his dismay.

One afternoon, Jacob and Nick received a visit from Alfonzo and Carmen. Jacob acted as if he was clueless, giving no indication that he even knew the two men. Carmen began the conversation.

"We've been following your company and have learned that you might be undergoing some financial difficulties. We represent some investors who see a lot of potential in J & N Manufacturing. They are interested in making you an offer to purchase your business."

Nick couldn't imagine where these two characters got word of the company's misfortunes...or could he?

"If you know the company isn't profitable, why would your investors want to buy it?"

"They have very deep pockets and see enormous potential for profits if the business is expanded. They have the means to do this."

Rattled by their visit, Nick said, "I'll think about your offer. Where can I reach you to tell you of my decision?"

"We'll contact you in a couple of days. We'll need a definite answer by then."

The men left abruptly, saying that they would be in touch.

"Where did that come from?" Nick asked Jacob with consternation.

Jacob answered, "I have no idea."

The company began losing more and more money. The bills kept piling up and there seemed to be a shortage of cash. It was all puzzling to Nick. New accounts were still coming in and the business should have been doing better than the books indicated.

A bounced check caught Nick's attention. *How could that be? We should have plenty of money in the account.* He went over to Jacob's disheveled desk, papers covering the surface. As he shuffled through the mass of paper, he saw that a number of their good vendors were not getting paid. He also found several collection letters threatening to cut off their credit.

Nick confronted Jacob with his discovery.

"Jacob, I don't understand what's going on. Why are we losing so much money?"

"If we'd bought that other supplier like I wanted, we wouldn't be in this situation."

"That's your answer to everything. Expand, expand, expand! Why aren't you ever satisfied? We have a good business here."

"If the business is so good, then why are we losing money?"

"I can't figure that out, but I'm going to get to the bottom of all of this."

That night, Nick stayed late and pored over the books. He discovered many irregularities in the bookkeeping, money missing, and the bogus vendors from which no actual items were purchased. The next day when Jacob came in the office, Nick waited for him... armed with all the information he'd uncovered.

"I was going over the books last night and learned what you've been doing."

"What are you talking about?"

"You've been cheating me. You've been cheating the business. I would have never expected this from you. You have done some despicable things, but skimming money?"

"Are you accusing me of skimming money from the business?"

"Yes, I am!"

"What kind of a person do you think I am?"

"I don't know you anymore. You've become a stranger."

"Nick, you don't understand."

"You're right. I don't understand. I don't understand how you could do this to me."

"I had no choice."

"Yes you did, and you chose to steal from me. Now get out of here."

"But, Nick..."

"Go!"

* * *

As he snapped back to the present, Jacob sat at the table with Howard in silence. Looking at Howard, ashamed, he said, "I can't talk about this anymore. I'm sure you think I am a despicable man, don't you."

"As I've said before...I'm not here to judge you. I'm here to help you."

"I was overcome with fear, greed, and my judgment was all messed up by the booze. I know that's not an excuse, but it's a reason."

"I'm now beginning to see why you are so troubled. Is there more you're not telling me?"

"After leaving Nick, I went home and hit the bottle for a few days. Nick called the police. Their investigation confirmed his accusations and I was arrested. In an effort to keep me quiet, Alfonzo and Carmen bailed me out. To preserve my reputation, I convincingly denied the charges. That's it. I can't go on."

"Jacob, you've come this far. Purge what's ailing you—all of it! Tell me the rest of the story, please."

"I can't. That's all I have to say."

"Sure you can. You need to be honest with me."

"That's it, Howard. That's all I can tell you!"

Jacob got up from the table, stormed to the front door, and slammed it behind him. Back out on the streets he went, leaving Howard wondering if he would ever see him again.

Chapter Nine

It had been raining for days, leaving Frankie miserable and cold, sitting in a wet and muddy foxhole hiding under his poncho to shield himself from the downpour. His throat stung and he suffered from a slight fever, both of which he tried to ignore. Showing vulnerability on the battlefield wasn't advisable. Like an injured animal, you stood out, making you easy prey. The cold rain leaked down the back of his neck, causing him to shiver. He adjusted his poncho and reached for a piece of paper in his chest pocket, a letter he'd received from Tom the day before. Carefully, he held it under his coat and began reading it for the third time.

Dear Frankie,

I hope this letter finds you in good health and spirits. Sorry I haven't written as much as I should. I'll try to do a better job of being a brother. I worry about you so, and I guess I try not to think about the fact that you are getting shot at every day. I may have to get another surgery on my bad leg. I hope it's not the case. I'll find out for sure next week. Not much new here other than that. Michael will be four years old the sixth of next month. We're planning a little party for him and his friends. Wish you could be here to enjoy it with us. Betty sends her love. Take care.

Love, Tom

Frankie worshiped his older brother. He missed the fun times they shared together, and he definitely yearned for Betty's cooking, an out-and-out contrast to the Army's C-rations, *that was for sure*. Folding the letter, he stuck it back in his shirt pocket. With a smile on his otherwise grim face, he began thinking of home and what he missed there, hoping Tom didn't need another surgery. He'd been through far too much agony with his leg over the years.

Frankie barely remembered the accident, nor did he remember much about his mother. Aside from the few photographs he'd seen of her, he could hardly recall what she even looked like. Likewise, he had few childhood memories of his father, and most of them engrained in his mind from the nasty rages about his father he heard from his aunt, uncle, and other members of the family. According to them, his father was a wicked and selfish man. Frankie's encounters with his father as an adult were few and far between. Their meetings were always interrupted by Tom yelling at his father to leave. Independent of the bad things he heard from family, and the few times they met, Frankie's recollection of his father was a blank. He had always wanted a relationship with him, but establishing one was a daunting task.

As he sat in the foxhole on this dismal day, he wondered about Jacob, and what had become of him since they last talked. *I would have liked to know him better*, he thought. He even contemplated looking him up when he got back from the war.

Suddenly they were hit with mortar fire. He frantically took cover as another soldier dove into the foxhole beside him.

"Dang, McCallum! Where'd that come from?" shouted Private Ben Cummings.

All around them soldiers ran for cover as more rounds exploded nearby.

"Move forward, men!" his sergeant hollered.

Frankie looked around; no one was moving.

"I said move forward!"

Suddenly, all the men were mobile. As he ran, Frankie took refuge behind some trees, or under whatever would provide him safe cover from the mortar fire. They advanced about seven hundred yards, then they were ordered to "dig in." The mortar rounds rang over their heads and exploded behind them. They stayed in their positions for about twenty minutes, but continued to get shelled.

"McCallum! Rogers! Sinclair! Go see if you can locate the mortars and radio back their positions," barked the sergeant.

"Yes sir!"

The three left the safety of their platoon and went out on patrol in search of the mortar placements. After about an hour, they located some German mortars.

"This is Fox Trot calling Range Finder."

"Ten-four."

Frankie radioed back the Germans' position, and it wasn't a minute before American artillery fire began raining down on them. The shelling was short of its mark, closer to Frank and his buddies than the enemy. The patrol retreated a few hundred yards then radioed back.

"You need to fire further down range! You're shelling us instead of the enemy!"

There was a barrage of more artillery fire. This time it hit its mark.

"Mission accomplished," Frankie advised the platoon leader.

★ ★ ★

Tom McCallum just machined his last part of the day. While cleaning up his area, the shop owner, Robert Quizdale, walked up to him with a man Tom didn't know.

"Hey, Tom?"

"Yes, Mr. Quizdale?"

"I'd like to introduce you to someone and talk with you for a moment."

"What is it?"

"This is Ed Miller. Ed, this is Tom McCallum."

The two shook hands.

"I was just telling Ed here that you are my best machinist."

"Well, thank you, Mr. Quizdale."

"You know I'm getting up in my years, and I've been looking for a buyer for my business. Ed is interested, so I thought he should meet you."

"Oh, I knew you were thinking about selling the place someday, but I didn't think you meant this soon."

"Well, Ed has made me a generous offer and I'm thinking he would be a good person to pass the business on to."

"Tom McCallum? You wouldn't be related to Jacob McCallum, would you?" Ed asked.

"Me? Oh, no. I've never heard of Jacob McCallum. With the same last name, we may be related somewhere along the line."

"I could have sworn he had a son named Tom, but I could be mistaken. Sad story about old Jacob." Ed shook his head. "He really made a mess of his life...his family's, too. Oh, well, I thought I'd ask anyway. If I bought the place, it would be for an investment. I'd need someone to run the business for me. Are you up for that?"

"Sure. Yeah. I'd be up for that."

"Good. Robert has told me a lot of good things about you."

Robert nodded his acknowledgment to Tom.

"We'll talk more about this another time. It was nice meeting you, Tom," Ed told him.

"It was nice to meet you, too."

While walking home from work, Tom reflected upon the conversation. Although he was flattered by Robert Quizdale recommending him to Ed Miller as a person who could run the shop, reservations surfaced regarding the sale of the business, and Mr. Miller's remarks about his father, and his questioning if Tom was Jacob's son.

As Tom opened the front door to his house, little Michael ran up and hugged his leg.

"Hey there, little buddy," Tom said as he picked up his son.

Betty greeted him with a kiss.

"You won't believe what I found out today."

"What's that?"

"Mr. Quizdale is selling the business."

"Really? How will that affect your job?"

"Well, Mr. Quizdale introduced me to the prospective buyer. Apparently, the guy is buying the business as an investment and he wants somebody to run it for him. Mr. Quizdale recommended me."

"That's wonderful!"

"I have some concerns, though."

"Concerns?"

"My father. The man knew my father and he wanted to know if I was his son."

"What did you tell him?"

"I told him I'd never heard of Jacob McCallum."

"Tom, you didn't."

"If he finds out I'm his son, he may not hire me. He knows my father's reputation. My father will haunt me from his grave."

Chapter Ten

After three more solid days of rain, the clouds parted and sunshine spilled over the bombed-out landscape. Frankie's platoon patrolled the area, sneaking through the forest in search of the enemy.

"Take five, men," the sergeant ordered, to the delight of the soldiers.

Leaning back against the trunk of a tree, Frankie kicked off his boots to give his feet a much-needed break.

"Ah, that feels so good," he said to his friend, PFC Marty Forman.

"Yeah, my feet are killing me, too," Marty responded.

"I can't wait for a couple of days of R and R."

"That would be nice right about now."

"How are things back home?" Frankie asked.

"Okay. But I sure do miss Ruth Ellen and my baby girl. I just got a letter from her and she sent me this picture of Sarah. Here, take a look."

Marty reached into his shirt pocket and showed Frankie a picture of his daughter.

"Wow, she sure is beautiful. Must take after her mother. Thank God she doesn't look like you," Frankie teased. "It won't be long before some guy will be knocking on the door and stealing her away from you."

"Hopefully I have a few years before that happens."

"Yeah, but time flies. And by the way, I pity the poor guy that comes knocking at your door to take your daughter on her first date."

"He better come armed," Marty joked. "Have you heard from your brother and sister?"

"Yeah, I got a letter from each of them just a few days ago. They're doing fine."

Frankie laid his head back and closed his eyes.

"I think I'm gonna try to get a few minutes of shut-eye."

The sun felt warm against Frankie's face. He dozed off rather quickly before being abruptly awakened by gunfire. Surrounded by German soldiers, Frankie grabbed his gun and took cover, returning fire. Overrun by the enemy, the sergeant radioed for backup. The firefight lasted about thirty minutes before a platoon of American soldiers flanked the Germans, delivering heavy casualties. Those left standing were taken prisoner.

★ ★ ★

The next day, Frankie's platoon snuck through the forest, trying to find a German artillery operation. It seemed like an easy enough mission, but they hadn't seen a German all day.

The sergeant commanded them to take a break. Frankie shed his helmet and took a seat on the ground next to Marty, where they resumed yesterday's conversation. Unexpectedly, a German sniper's rifle discharged. The bullet passed through Frankie's head and he slumped to the ground. The men scurried for cover and began firing in the direction of the sniper, who managed to slip away. Marty leaned over and covered Frankie's body, which lay motionless on the ground, blood gushing from the wound.

"Frankie! Frankie!"

Other soldiers pulled Marty off Frankie's body. One of the soldiers said gently, "He's gone, Marty. He's gone."

★ ★ ★

About a week later, Tom and Betty were enjoying the quiet of their evening when there was a knock at the door.

"I'll get it," Tom said.

"Who could it be at this time of night?" Betty asked.

"I have a telegram for a Mr. Tom McCallum."

"That's me."

The gentleman handed Tom a piece of paper. Then he turned and walked away.

Tom opened the envelope.

We regret to inform you that Private First Class Frank McCallum was fatally wounded while on patrol in Germany in service to his country and the United States Army. Details to follow in letter.

Tom dropped the telegram, standing there, stunned.

Betty walked up behind him. "Who was it?"

She saw the tears streaming from Tom's eyes as he trembled. Without saying a word, he went straight to their bedroom. Betty bent over and picked up the piece of paper, which was lying on the floor. She read it and screamed, "Not Frankie. No!"

Immediately, she ran into the bedroom, where Tom sat on the edge of the bed, his head cradled in his hands, weeping. She knelt before him and they clung to each other.

Finally, Tom spoke. "He really never even had a chance to experience life."

"He was so young, so innocent," Betty murmured.

"I just knew this was going to happen. I prayed so hard that it wouldn't."

Betty looked up at Tom, searching for any appropriate words. Thinking of none, she held him close. He gently moved Betty's arms away, got up off the bed, and walked over to the window, where he peered out into the night. She came up behind him and wrapped both of her arms around his waist.

"Oh, Tom...I'm so sorry."

He turned to face her, his face wrinkled in pain as he tried to speak. She gently put her finger to his quivering lips. He kissed her hand and they embraced again, holding each other while they both stood, sobbing.

"I can't bear to tell our little Michael...and Emma. What am I going to say?"

"I know it's going to be difficult, but you must be strong."

"I'll send Emma a telegram first thing in the morning. We'll need to make arrangements as soon as we learn the details."

Tom and Betty spent the night talking about it, and at times finding solace in their fond memories of family time with Frankie. They even managed a laugh or two as they recounted stories about his life. Hours of grief, several pots of coffee, and many tears later, they fell asleep together on the living room sofa, Betty's head resting on Tom's chest.

The morning sun crept through the living room window and finally into Tom's weary eyes, slowly awakening him. He lay still, mindful of Betty still soundly sleeping, her body pressing tightly against his. He wished it had all been a terrible dream, but he quickly came to the realization that it wasn't. Careful not to awaken Betty, he gently moved her head, placing it on the soft pillow at the end of the sofa.

Walking straight to the coffeepot, Tom prepared some fresh coffee. The sound of it percolating and the scent of the steaming grinds stirred Betty awake. She rose slowly from the sofa and joined Tom in the kitchen, sitting next to him at the table. Taking a sip of coffee, Tom said sadly, "I still can't believe it." It just seemed so unreal, so raw. He thought, agonizingly, about the daunting tasks before him, telling Emma and Michael, making funeral arrangements, and doing all the things that went into dealing with a death in the family. They discussed it all with dread and sorrow.

Tom didn't even bother to change clothes, or comb his hair, before leaving for the Western Union office. He was numb, except for the aching feeling that weighed heavily in his heart. After carefully considering the words he would send in the telegram to Emma, he handed the note to the telegraph operator, who read it then looked up at Tom with sympathy.

On the way home, he stopped by work to tell his boss he wouldn't be coming to work that day. Robert was more than understanding, telling him to take the rest of the week off, with pay.

Later that afternoon, there was a knock at Emma's door. A cheerful gentleman greeted her, obviously unaware of the heart-breaking news contained in the envelope he held in his hand. He tipped his hat and bid her a good day. She closed the door and leaned against it as she tore open the envelope. The words stung her heart. She walked over to the table, where she sat down and read it again, now fully comprehending what it said. Crumpling it up into a ball, she pounded her fist on the table before laying her head down and wailing.

Weeks passed before Tom heard any more news from the Department of War. Frankie's body made its journey back to Chicago and Tom made the final preparations for his funeral. Tom and Emma decided to bury Frankie next to their mother.

The rains poured from the heavens that day. A small gathering of family and friends huddled together under umbrellas at the gravesite. A contingency of soldiers gave Frankie his final salute. Seven of them stood in line at attention, then in unison, they raised their rifles and fired three times into the sky. The flag was removed from his coffin, folded with precision, and handed to Tom and Emma. They all stayed until the attendants lowered Frankie's casket into his grave. His mother's gravesite overflowed with flowers for the somber occasion, adding the only color on this otherwise drab day.

Chapter Eleven

After walking the streets, Jacob calmed down to the point where he began thinking rationally again. He contemplated returning to the mission, but feared Howard would shun him. Instead, he sank down onto a bench to rest a spell while he pondered what to do. Overcome with a nagging feeling he should return to the mission, he rose and began walking in that direction. On his way, he thought about his budding relationship with God, and his journey toward forgiveness. For this, he desperately needed Howard's assistance.

The following morning Jacob felt much better after enjoying a good night's sleep. There were no nightmares, not even any pleasant dreams. Seeking out Howard, he found him walking down the hall.

"I didn't think I would ever see you again," Howard said.

"I was sure you wouldn't. But after hours of prayer I decided to come back. Can you ever forgive me?"

"I have nothing for which to forgive you. What you told me is in your past. I want to help you with the present and the future."

Jacob began to speak, then hesitated.

"What is it, Jacob?"

"Last night made me come to the realization that I need to find Tom and Frankie. I'm ready to ask them for their forgiveness. Will you come with me for support?"

"Today?"

"Right now, while I have the courage. Besides, it's Saturday and Tom should be home."

"Sure I will. But where will you begin looking for them? Chicago's a big place."

"When I searched for them, I met a woman who lives at their last address. She said the landlord might have Tom's forwarding address. The landlord wasn't home when I tried to speak with him."

"Let me grab my jacket and we'll go."

Howard and Jacob set out to talk with the landlord in hopes he could give Jacob the information that would lead them to Tom and Frankie. When they arrived at the landlord's home, an elderly woman was sweeping the front porch. Jacob stopped at the bottom of the steps and called out to her.

"Excuse me. I'm looking for a Mr. Schmidt."

"I'm Mrs. Schmidt. How can I help you?"

"I'm trying to locate my son, who used to live down the street at 1641. The woman who lives there now said your husband may have my son's address."

She invited them inside, introducing them to her husband. Mr. Schmidt was tall and skinny with a head of thick, uncombed hair. He wore blue suspenders to hold up his baggy pants.

"Thomas McCallum?" the man asked to be sure.

"Yes," Jacob replied.

"How long ago would it have been?"

"About two years ago, maybe?" Jacob wasn't quite sure.

The man licked his thumb and began leafing through a thick pile of papers he pulled from a file.

"Thomas McCallum...let's see."

Jacob and Howard anxiously looked over his shoulder. The man tugged on his suspenders, then slipped his glasses down on his nose.

"Ah. Here we go. Thomas McCallum. Actually, he moved not far from here, just a few blocks up on Wabash."

Scribbling the address on a piece of paper, he handed it to Jacob.

"Thank you, sir."

"I hope this helps you," the man replied.

Jacob and Howard walked slowly down the street in the direction of Tom's address.

"Are you up for this today, Jacob?"

"I'm not sure. I'm really not sure at all."

Sensing Jacob's vulnerability, Howard spoke up. "I don't know, Jacob. Maybe it's not a good idea to do this today. Perhaps we should return to the mission and discuss a strategy as to how to approach the situation, given the volatile nature of your relationship with your sons."

"No, I want to get this over with, one way or the other. I need to do it today."

They proceeded on their journey.

"What should I say when I see them?"

"Simply tell them you're sorry and that you want to speak with them about your feelings and to ask for their forgiveness."

"But what if they say no?"

"How much does all this mean to you?"

"It means everything. If I can gain the love and acceptance of my children after what I've done to them, I will never ask for anything else."

"Well, then, I guess you will have to take a chance if you want the answer."

As they approached the address Mr. Schmidt had given him, Jacob began to contemplate what lay ahead. *What if they throw me out?* His mind raced. He craved a drink. Satan was ribbing him…he could feel it. As Jacob walked, his knees felt weak with apprehension. They passed a grassy spot and Jacob stopped.

"I need to sit down for a bit."

They relaxed at the base of an old oak tree, remaining there for a few more minutes while Jacob gathered his wits.

"Let's get this over with," Jacob said as he stood.

They made their way to the address on the piece of paper. As they stood across the street from 4473 Wabash, Jacob's stomach churned.

"Do you want me to stay here?" Howard asked.

"No! If I ever needed a friend's support, this is the time."

They crossed the street and Jacob stood at the front door. Suddenly, he lost his nerve and took a few steps back. Feeling ill-prepared, Jacob backed away, taking a seat on a bench across the street.

Howard, void of any words of reassurance, took a seat next to Jacob and remained silent. Jacob stared at Tom's front door, knowing he lacked the courage to do what he came to do. A little more than an hour passed.

The door to the house opened. A tall, handsome young man emerged. It was Tom, the spitting image of Jacob when he was younger. Jacob watched as Tom limped down the street, out of sight. After witnessing his son's awkward limp, Jacob turned to Howard and shook his head.

It was about twenty minutes before Tom returned. He juggled several bags of groceries in his arms as he opened the front door to his home. Jacob rose from the bench and started to cross the street. Dazed by the prospect of talking with his sons, he stepped off the curb...

"Jacob! Look out!" Howard shouted.

The sound of a car horn blared, followed by the piercing noise of screeching tires. Jacob looked up and saw the approaching car, freezing in his tracks. Howard tried to save his friend, but was too late. The car slid toward Jacob and stopped just a foot short of hitting him.

"Are you okay?" a man yelled as he exited his car.

"Yeah, sure, I'm fine. I just wasn't thinking and walked out in the street without looking."

"He'll be okay," Howard reassured him. "I'll take care of him. You can go about your business."

"That was close," Howard said as he reached for Jacob's arm. The near miss left Jacob breathless.

"I can't do this. Not today," Jacob said in a tone of disappointment.

Lacking the nerve to knock on Tom's door, Jacob abruptly turned and walked back toward the Salvation Army Mission. Howard followed. After several blocks, Jacob told Howard he wanted to be alone.

"Are you going to be all right?"

"I'll be okay. I just need to walk and be by myself for a while. I've got some thinking to do."

Howard obliged, leaving him to his thoughts. Jacob walked around town without purpose. Along the way, he passed several taverns, each beckoning him in for a drink. As he approached a bar on the corner of 4th and Washington, he slowed. Looking through the window, he watched as the patrons laughed and enjoyed the festive atmosphere. The door swung open and Jacob got a whiff of the interior. It was tremendously inviting.

No, he thought to himself. *That would be a bad idea.*

Jacob quickly walked away, but after about ten paces, he turned and walked back to the tavern. He stood in front of the plate glass window. Suddenly, he saw his reflection. Staring at himself in the glass, he came to the recurring conclusion that his life was a worthless mess, a rationalization that caused him to open the door and enter the tavern, where he took a seat at the bar.

"Give me a glass of whiskey."

"Coming right up," the bartender replied.

Jacob took a quick swig, then carefully set the glass back on the top of the bar. He stared at it curiously. It didn't taste the same. It didn't satisfy him as it had always done in the past. He raised the glass to his lips again and took another swallow. Gazing at the glass of booze, he felt guilty…ashamed. He stood and set the glass back on the bar. Sliding off his stool, he departed, leaving the half-filled glass of whiskey behind.

When he returned to the mission, Howard eagerly greeted him.

"Where have you been?"

"I just was walking around. I have something to confess to you."

Jacob's face was awash with shame.

"Yes?"

"While I was walking, I strolled by a bar and couldn't resist the urge to go inside for a drink."

"Oh, Jacob—no."

"I ordered a glass of whiskey and took a drink. It tasted terrible. My shame and guilt caused me to set the glass back on the bar and leave without finishing it. Satan was testing me, but I passed the test," he said grimly.

"I'm so proud of you."

"Proud? I slipped up and had a drink."

"Yes, but you knew it was the wrong thing to do and you had the courage to put the drink down and walk away. You've come a long way, Jacob."

Chapter Twelve

A few days later, Jacob and Howard set out to visit Tom and Frankie again. They made it back to the bench where they had sat before. Jacob attempted to garner the nerve to confront his sons, sitting quietly, staring at the house in a trance, fearful of what awaited him. His thoughts drifted back to when he took Tom fishing for the first time.

"Now hold the rod still and watch the bobbin."

"What's a bobbin, Papa?"

"It's that red and white thing floating out there on the water. When a fish bites, it will pull the bobbin under. When that happens, pull back on the rod like this to set the hook."

Jacob showed Tom the proper technique, then enjoyed the spectacle of watching his six-year-old son master the art of fishing.

"Papa! Papa! I've got one. I've got one!"

Tom reeled frantically. Jacob smiled at the wonder on Tom's face when he got the first glimpse of what was at the end of his line, a whopping six-inch sunfish, which Tom proudly displayed.

The noise of a passing streetcar brought Jacob back to the

present and extinguished the bright smile from his face. Sitting on the bench across the street from his sons, he felt estranged from their love. He wondered about all the delightful memories he'd squandered.

Realizing it was time, he motioned for Howard to join him as he walked across the street. Jacob took a deep breath and knocked on the door, his chest clinched tight. Tom opened the door. Upon seeing Jacob, a horrified look crossed his face, which quickly turned to one of anger. Jacob and Tom stood, just a few feet apart, staring at one another. Tom was first to speak.

"How did you find me? What do you want?"

"Tom, I...I came to say I'm sorry. I'm—"

"Don't you think it's a little late for that?"

"I was hoping not."

"Well, you're much too late. Too much time has passed, too much has happened for you to just walk in here, say you're sorry, and make everything all right. Things will never be all right between us. You're just a murdering bum."

"I realize I haven't been the ideal father and I've done some revolting things, but I just want the chance to show you and Frankie how sorry I am. Please give me a chance."

"You had your chance. I want nothing to do with you. I've told you this before."

"What about Frankie? I'd like to talk to him."

"Oh, you'd like to talk to Frankie, would you? Well, like I said, it's too late!"

"Why don't you let Frankie decide that for himself? I'd like to speak with him. Is he still living with you?"

Tom's face shuddered and turned a deep shade of crimson. His upper lip snarled, his eyes filling with tears.

"That's my point! Frankie is not living with me...he's not living at all. Frankie is dead!"

"Dead?"

"Dead! You got that? Frankie's dead!"

"But...how? When?"

"We buried him a few months ago. He got shot by a German sniper while fighting in Europe."

"My God, Frankie?" Jacob was crushed and he immediately began to weep.

"Spare me your tears, you pathetic old man. We couldn't even find you to tell you."

"Tommy, please..."

Tom couldn't contain his rage any longer. Deep creases broke out on his forehead; his eyes widened wildly while the veins bulged from the thin skin on his neck. He screamed, "I want nothing to do with you! Do you understand that? As far as I'm concerned, you can drop dead!"

The door slammed. The reunion was over just as quickly as it began, leaving Jacob gasping for air. He melted into the cement steps, lying there weeping, while Howard tried to comfort him and pull him away from the door. Howard, too, appeared dazed by what he had seen and heard.

Howard ushered Jacob up the street, away from Tom's house. Jacob began wheezing, finding it difficult to breathe.

"I've got to stop," he told Howard as he panted.

Finding the refuge of a light pole for support, he grabbed it, holding on as tight as he could. His grip was too weak to support him. He let his hands slide down the pole until his body slumped to the ground.

"Frankie. Oh, my Frankie. I'm so sorry." He surrendered

himself to the ground, where he lay on his back and wept despondently.

Howard put his hands on Jacob's shoulders.

"I just want to die. Leave me alone."

"I'm so sorry, Jacob."

"Why did God let this happen? Why didn't he take my worthless life and spare Frankie's?"

"Please don't blame God for this. You must have faith."

"Take me back, Howard. Take me back home."

As they walked back to the mission, Jacob was silent. Something he'd said earlier stuck in Howard's mind. Jacob called the mission "home," an indication that Jacob had a sense of belonging in his life. When they reached the mission, Jacob went straight to his cot, where he cried himself to sleep.

* * *

Jacob slept until around 9 p.m., when he awakened. Immediately, troubling thoughts came to his mind as he lay there considering taking his own life. This, he felt, would finally offer him the peace he desired. Craving a smoke and a drink, he snuck out the front door of the mission and headed for the closest tavern. Slapping what little money he possessed down hard on the bar, he ordered a drink. As the bartender poured it into a glass, the sweet fragrance of the whiskey fueled his desire. Wasting little time, he chugged it down, banging the glass down on the bar.

"I'll have another."

After hours of hard drinking and chain-smoking, Jacob ran out of money. Still craving more, he stole a bottle from the bar and staggered out the door unnoticed. He wended his way back to the mission, all the while sipping from the stolen bottle of booze. Quietly closing the door, he turned and discovered Howard standing behind him. Though Howard empathized with Jacob's situation, he was disappointed to the point of being angry.

"We have rules here. One of which is our residents are not allowed to come back here if they're drunk. And if a resident brings alcohol into the mission, they are automatically tossed out. What were you thinking?"

Irritated, Jacob shouted, "So throw me out then! I don't care. I don't care about anything."

Howard snatched the bottle from Jacob's hand.

"Come in and sit down."

"Why should I?"

"We need to talk. The answer isn't in this bottle, it isn't on the streets, it's within you."

Howard walked over to a table and sat down, waiting for Jacob to join him. Jacob remained at the front door, indecisive about whether to return to the streets and drink himself to death or to join Howard at the table. This would be a defining moment in Jacob's life. Howard had a dire look of concern. Jacob was drunk and full of rage. He stood looking at the door then back at Howard.

"Please come over here and sit down. We'll have a talk about all of this."

Jacob opened the door and stepped out onto the sidewalk, slamming the door behind him. Howard's lip drew taut as he shook his head in disappointment. *Jacob had come so close*, he thought. It crossed his mind to go after him, but Howard's experience with alcoholics led him to be patient. *Maybe after he sobers up, he'll come to his senses.*

Suddenly the door swung open and Jacob stepped back inside. Walking over to the table, he asked, "Are you going to toss me out?"

"Going by the rules, I have to. But on the other hand, if this incident never happened, it wouldn't be an issue." Howard paused for a moment, looking down at his feet. He looked up with a compassionate smile and said, "Let's just say it never happened. But you have to promise me that you will never do this again. The choice is yours, Jacob. I want to help you. But to help anyone, that person needs to admit he can't do it alone and that he needs help."

Jacob snapped back angrily, "Howard, what do you know about all of this? You're a pastor. You've always been on the right side of things. You've never gone through what I have, or what anyone in this place has. You've never been squeezed by the tight grip of booze. You have never been in a state of mind where you don't want to live any longer. You just don't understand."

Howard reached over the table and grabbed Jacob by his shirt, lifting him from his chair. He yanked him halfway across the table, catapulting Jacob's chair across the room.

Howard shook with anger and shouted, "I don't understand? You think I don't understand? You don't know anything about me or my past. I was just like you, Jacob. A lost drunk, wandering around the streets looking for my next drink...my next smoke, sleeping in gutters and flophouses. So don't tell me I don't understand, because I do! Don't ever tell me that again."

Howard released Jacob from his grasp. His emotional admission sobered Jacob, who retrieved his chair and sat back down at the table.

"Calm down, Howard. I would have never even imagined—"

Howard interrupted him. "Well, now you know my dirty little secret. I have walked where you have. I do understand. Now, are you going to let me help you, or are you going to walk out that door and destroy your life . . . what's left of it? If you want to rot in hell, be my guest."

"Howard, I can't deal with all of this."

"You won't be going through it alone, I can assure you."

"Frankie's dead. He's dead, and I didn't even know it. Why? Why my Frankie?"

"That's a question that you, as a mere human, will never be able to comprehend. You can be proud of Frankie that he died defending his country. He's a hero. Jacob, I'm very sorry about how things ended with you and Tom today. And I'm certainly sorry that you lost Frankie. I know it was a devastating blow, but you can't let this distract you. It's obvious that Tom is unreceptive to seeing you or forgiving you. Perhaps in time he may change his mind."

"I don't think that will ever be the case."

"That may be, but at this point it seems like that's Tom's choice. Perhaps God will work on his heart, and in the future he'll be more receptive. Jacob, I think you've been leaving out a very important part of your story."

"What do you mean?"

"Tom referred to you as a murderer. What was that all about?"

Jacob went silent. "I don't want to discuss it."

"Dang it! You have to. You've bared your soul in order to relieve your conscience of this weight you've been carrying for all these years. Now level with me, Jacob."

Jacob thought for a moment before deciding it was time to come clean...to reveal the deep secret that haunted his innermost being.

"My life was on a very slippery slope. My drinking, carousing, and the men I was associated with destroyed my relationship with Amanda."

Jacob opened up and began to tell Howard everything...the details of his misery, and why his children hated him so.

"After my arrest, I called Amanda and pleaded with her to bring the children and come back home. I told her I was innocent and that I'd changed my ways...that I had stopped drinking. I wanted to make it all up to her. I guess she felt sorry for me and she did as I asked. I tried my best to stop drinking, and for a while I did. We were getting along great. We had fallen back in love again. Then I began to slip back into my old ways. And something terrible happened on New Year's Eve in 1922. The night started off badly. It ended in a way that forever changed my life. On that night I lost everything that was left in my life, the important things: Amanda and my children."

"Tell me how."

"This is going to be very difficult for me to relive."

"You must go on, Jacob. It's the only way."

Howard grasped Jacob's hands in support. Jacob closed his eyes and placed himself back on that snowy New Year's Eve so many years ago.

* * *

"Amanda...are you ready yet?"

"I don't even want to go."

"Come on, it'll be fun. The Marshalls were nice enough to invite us to their dinner party. It would be rude not to go."

"Since when have you worried about being rude?"

"Can't you just relax and have a good time?"

"That's just it, your idea of a good time and mine are totally different. Look at you, you've had four or five drinks and we're not even at the party yet. You're drunk already."

"I'll be okay. I'm just celebrating a little early, that's all."

"You always have some excuse for your behavior. You promised me you would stop drinking. That's a big part of why I came back. Now look at you."

"Amanda, look around at all you have. I gave it to you."

"I would trade every bit of this just to have my old Jacob back."

"Come here, Amanda."

"Why should I?"

"Because I love you and I want to give you a kiss."

"Your breath reeks of alcohol. I want no part of it."

"Come on, just a little kiss."

Amanda relented and slowly walked over to Jacob.

"You look beautiful in that dress," Jacob said as he held both of her hands in front of him.

She looked up at him and smiled. "You look pretty handsome yourself in that tuxedo."

Jacob pulled her toward him and embraced her. "Let's stop all this bickering. I love you so much."

"I love you, too, Jacob. But we have been over this a million times before. You know how I feel about your drinking. I can't put up with it."

"I'm sorry, dear. I've tried to stop, but it is difficult for me."

"Well, if you want things to work out between us, you're going to have to try harder. I'll help you any way I can, but I refuse to go on if you continue to drink."

"I'll try, Amanda. I love you too much not to."

"Let's just stay home tonight, Jacob—can we?"

"It's important that we go. There will be some good contacts there."

"I want to stay home and snuggle. Besides, if we go, you'll be tempted to drink."

"I promise I won't have a thing to drink if we go."

"You promise?"

"Yes."

"You promise to turn your life around?"

"I will."

Amanda stood on her tiptoes and gently kissed Jacob on the lips.

"I hope this is the last time I smell alcohol on your breath."

"It will be . . . I promise. Now let's get going; the children are getting restless."

Jacob loaded the children into the car. Amanda reluctantly opened the passenger side door and climbed in. Jacob slid into the plush seat of his 1922 Cadillac, adjusted his coat, then he started the car and they took off for the party.

"Will Timmy and Bobby be there tonight?" Tommy asked.

"Yeah, and there'll be a lot of other children there for all of you to play with. It'll be fun to ring in the New Year."

When they arrived at the Marshalls', Jacob was anxious to get the party started.

"Come on, Amanda, let's go in."

"Let me fix my makeup."

"You look fantastic. Come on."

Jacob gave her a few minutes before entering the house. They were greeted warmly by all in attendance. Despite his business indiscretions, Jacob was still acknowledged as a quasi-celebrity.

"Would you like a cocktail before dinner, Jacob?" the host offered.

Amanda gave Jacob a stern look.

"No thank you. I'm just fine."

"Oh, come on, it's New Year's Eve. Just one to loosen you up a little."

"I'm loose enough. I had a few before we left the house."

Jacob and Amanda circulated among the crowd, greeting old friends and meeting new ones. The drink offers kept coming Jacob's way. Though tempted, he refused all the invitations. At dinner, a wineglass filled with red wine sat next to his and Amanda's plates. Before dinner, the host, Robert Marshall, stood at the head of the table and proposed a toast.

"To great friendships and to a prosperous new year for all my friends here tonight, I propose this toast."

Jacob picked up his glass, looking at Amanda for her approval. He didn't get it. Instead he got a steely glare, which served as a warning for him to put the glass back in its place. Jacob thought for a moment and then rationalized to himself that it was just a friendly glass of wine, and it shouldn't count as actually drinking. He participated in the toast and continued to sip the remainder of the wine in his glass throughout dinner. Then he had another. After dinner, Amanda asked Jacob to join her in the foyer.

"I can't believe you."

"What?"

"Don't act stupid with me! You know what I mean."

"Seriously, I don't."

"What did we talk about just before leaving the house to come here?"

"Surely you're not talking about the wine I had with dinner?"

"That is exactly what I'm talking about!"

"Amanda, it was just a couple of harmless glasses of wine to accentuate the taste of the meal."

"There is nothing harmless about alcohol where you're concerned. You promised me you would stop drinking. Here it is a few hours after your promise and you have already broken it."

"I don't consider having a glass of wine as drinking."

"Then what is it? It isn't like it was grape juice...it was alcohol."

"I think you're being a bit ridiculous."

"Oh, am I? I just want to go home. I'm not feeling well."

"But we haven't even rung in the New Year."

"You want to stay here for the New Year? Is that so you can have another toast with champagne...or who knows what?"

"It's not like I'm staggering drunk or anything."

"You *are* drunk! But that's not the point. In my book, a promise is a promise. Don't you understand the trouble alcohol has caused our marriage...and your business?"

"It's not like that, Amanda. It was just a little wine."

"That's where it begins. It ends with you drinking more and more until you are obnoxiously drunk. You can't drink, Jacob. You can't drink at all if you are sincere about getting sober. Don't you understand that?"

Jacob looked at her and shook his head.

"If you want to stay here and ring in the New Year with your friends, go ahead. I'm calling a cab and taking the children home. I have a headache and I want to leave. Which is more important to you, Jacob...me, or your alcohol? You choose!"

"You are, of course."

"Then let's go home before something terrible happens."

Jacob thought for a moment, sighed, and then agreed to leave the party.

"Okay, have it your way. We'll leave, but I think the Marshalls will consider it a snub."

"I don't actually care what they think. I'll tell them I am feeling ill, and that will be our excuse to leave."

Jacob went to retrieve their coats and round up the children while Amanda sought out Robert and Melissa Marshall to politely excuse her family from the party.

"I'm very sorry you have to leave before the fun starts."

"We are also, but I am not feeling well. Thank you for your hospitality. The dinner was delicious."

Jacob closed his car door, still in disbelief that Amanda would get so upset about him having a few glasses of wine. After several minutes in the car, he revisited the subject, but Amanda refused to discuss it further. Jacob decided to let it pass. He wanted to say something to make amends, but nothing of value came to mind. As he looked in the rearview mirror, he noticed Tommy, Frankie, and Emma asleep in the backseat.

"Look at our angels back there," he said to break the ice.

Amanda turned to see the children.

"They sure are cute."

"Look, Amanda...I'm sorry about tonight."

"You should be."

"Come over here." Jacob beckoned her to sit next to him on the bench seat.

"We're not teenagers, for heaven sakes." She laughed.

"Come here."

Amanda accommodated him, moving closer.

"Let's not argue. I just slipped up a little bit, that's all."

"There is no excuse for your behavior."

"All right. I know that. I'm sorry and it won't happen again."

"Okay, you're forgiven. But don't let it ever happen again."

"When we get home, we'll put the kids to bed, then we'll snuggle on the sofa."

"That's what I wanted to do all along."

"I should have listened to you in the first place."

"Yeah, you should have," Amanda teased.

Jacob put his arm around her and drew her close. She kissed him softly on the cheek. The anticipation of a quiet New Year's celebration with her true love made her eager to get home. It had been several years since they'd shared any real intimacy. Jacob welcomed her excitement as he sped along.

"Slow down, honey!"

"I want to get home and share this night with you. Just listen to that engine purr."

"Jacob! It's not safe. Slow down."

Accelerating as he approached a turn in the road, he didn't see the sheet of black ice. The car skidded off the road, struck a tree, and then spun violently before overturning and coming to rest against another tree, upright.

The screaming coming from the car just before impact was replaced by a sudden silence. Jacob pushed himself away from the steering wheel, blood dripping from his forehead. His ears were still ringing; shattered glass was everywhere. He could faintly hear Tommy moaning. He had been thrown from the backseat and hit the dashboard. He now lay on the front passenger side floor, seriously injured. Jacob gathered his wits, checked on Tommy, then opened the rear door to check on Frankie and Emma. Though shaken, they were all right.

"Amanda. Amanda! Where are you?"

Amanda was gone from the front seat. Had she walked away? Jacob frantically searched for her.

"Amanda!"

His heart stopped momentarily as he looked down the embankment and saw Amanda's body. She had been thrown from the car. When he reached her, she was lifeless. Her face was crushed unrecognizably from the impact, her torso mangled from being run over by the car after she was ejected.

"My God! No! Amanda, please come back to me. Please!"

Jacob held Amanda's cold body against his chest and screamed.

"Is Mommy all right, Daddy?" Frankie called out.

"Stay up there, son. Don't come down here."

Headlights shined around the corner as a car approached. A man and his wife stopped to offer assistance. The woman took Frankie and Emma back to her car to comfort them.

"Are Mommy and Tommy okay?" Frankie kept asking.

"They'll be fine," she said to pacify him.

The man ran over to the passenger side of the car and saw Tommy, who by now had rolled out onto the ground. The bone in his right leg had pierced the skin and he was bleeding profusely.

"Sir, are you hurt?" the man yelled down to Jacob.

"No, it's my wife."

The man sprinted through the snow to reach them. He found Jacob cradling Amanda's upper body, his coat red with her blood. Jacob was in shock.

"She's gone, sir."

"No, she can't be."

The man had to pull Jacob off her.

"Your son's in bad shape. If we don't get him some help, he'll bleed to death."

* * *

Howard felt his eyes well with tears. Jacob was in terrible pain. He sat there, sobbing uncontrollably.

"I can't go on. This is too hard," he told Howard.

"You must. You need to cleanse your soul of these festering wounds. You've come this far, Jacob, now tell me the rest of your story."

Jacob continued, "As we attended to Tommy, I could hear Frankie and Emma screaming for their mother, and calling out to Tommy. Tommy's leg was all mangled and bleeding. He was unconscious. If it weren't for the fact he was bleeding, I would have sworn he was dead. We tied a makeshift tourniquet around his leg and moved him to the man's car then drove Tommy, Frankie, and Emma to the hospital. I stayed behind with Amanda. Out of respect, I covered her face with my coat and waited for the police to arrive. It was the longest half hour of my life. When they finally got there, they took control of the scene and called an ambulance for Amanda. As the police questioned me, they smelled the alcohol on my breath so they arrested me. Tommy almost lost his leg. Amanda was buried a few days after New Year's. I wasn't able to attend the funeral, or visit Tommy in the hospital, where he remained for months. I sat behind bars awaiting trial on manslaughter charges and for the embezzlement beef. I was convicted of both and sentenced to ten years, and served the full sentence. I wish they had sentenced me to death."

"What happened to your children?"

"Amanda's sister and husband raised them. While in prison, the haze of alcoholism lifted from my head and I came to realize what I had lost. This was an agonizing time for me. Just about every night, my sleep was pierced with nightmares about the accident. I was released from prison on February 4, 1932. We were in the middle of the Great Depression. Initially, I tried to reunite with my children. Tommy and Emma refused to see me, and Amanda's sister wouldn't let me near Frankie. I was driven away by shame. To cope, I returned to the bottle, drifting aimlessly around the country, hopping freight trains from town to town, taking odd jobs and even begging at times to get by. My children grew up with an image of me painted by bitter relatives and friends…one of a drunk, a bum, and a murderer. Frankie barely had his own memory of me."

Jacob began to weep again, but felt a terrific sense of relief that he had finally told Howard everything he'd been withholding since the day they met.

"It's all right. Everything will be all right, my friend. I think we've done all we can here tonight. Why don't we turn in and get some sleep."

* * *

Over morning coffee, Jacob informed Howard of his plans to travel to Baltimore in an attempt to locate his daughter.

"But you don't even know where she lives, or if she's still in Baltimore."

"I know. But I've got to try and find her."

"Jacob, I'm worried about you. I don't think it's wise for you to leave right now. You've been through a lot in the last few days. Being rejected by Tom, and finding out about Frankie, was traumatic. You should give it some time before trying to approach Emma."

"There is nothing left here for me. I have one more shot at recapturing a small portion of my previous life. That opportunity is in Baltimore, with Emma, not here."

"But what if she rejects you?"

"Well...then I guess I have no reason to go on in life. They can donate my body to science!"

"That's awfully grim...another good reason why you should remain here for a while."

"Well...that's just the way it is. I've made my decision. I can't take it any longer."

"If you insist, let me set you up with a friend of mine in Baltimore. His name is Bob Parsley, and he heads a Salvation Army Mission there. Here...I'll write down his address for you. Look him up when you get there. You can stay at his mission until you get on your feet. Stay here just a few more days and let me make the arrangements in Baltimore."

"I appreciate the help. Thank you."

Howard phoned his friend, Bob Parsley, and told him about

Jacob and his troubled life. He asked Bob to look after Jacob and to help him as much as he could. For the next few days, Jacob and Howard spoke little of Jacob's dilemma. For the first time since they met, they were able to share a few laughs and enjoyed their remaining time together.

After church service one night, Jacob asked Howard if he could have a word with him.

"What is it, Jacob?"

"I just wanted to thank you for being my friend and for all you have done for me. I will never forget you, Howard."

"What? Is this some kind of a good-bye?"

"Yes. I'll be leaving early tomorrow morning."

"Why so soon?"

"We've been through all of that. I have to find Emma."

"At least, let's have breakfast tomorrow, and then you can be on your way. I've phoned Bob Parsley and he is expecting you. Here, I bought you a train ticket to Baltimore."

"Oh, I can't accept that. Besides, you can't afford such a thing."

"It's okay. I have been saving my money for a special occasion or purpose such as this. It is my parting gift to you. Please take it, my friend."

"Well, thank you. But it isn't necessary."

"So I'll see you at breakfast?"

"Sure, Howard, tomorrow we'll have breakfast," Jacob said with a wink.

★ ★ ★

Howard got up early and went to the dining hall to look for Jacob, but he was nowhere to be found. *Has he overslept?*

Howard thought. He went to Jacob's cot, expecting to find him asleep. When he arrived, he found that Jacob's bed was neatly made, an envelope resting on the pillow with Howard's name inscribed on it. Howard opened the envelope, which contained a note and the train ticket he had given to Jacob. The note read:

Dear Howard,

I'm not good at good-byes, so I decided to skip breakfast and write you this note instead. I can never thank you adequately for your friendship, or for all you have taught me about myself. You have given me faith and hope that I can make something positive happen in the life I have remaining. I hope I will see you again, but if not... know you will always be in my heart and in my thoughts.

Your friend,
Jacob

P.S. Thank you very much for the train ticket, but I am returning it so you can cash it in and get your money back. No offense, but I prefer traveling first class. There is much more room in a boxcar to stretch out and relax.

A smile graced Howard's face. He shook his head in amusement and said aloud, "Jacob, Jacob, Jacob."

* * *

A cold wind swept the fallen leaves across the ground at Jacob's feet. He stood in the middle of a cemetery, looking down at a tombstone with the inscription: FRANK MCCALLUM. DIED IN SERVICE TO HIS COUNTRY. Next to Frankie's grave was a tombstone that read: AMANDA MCCALLUM. Jacob was in prison for Amanda's funeral, and had no idea she and Frankie were buried side by side.

Sadly, he knelt. "Amanda, Frankie...I am so sorry I failed you. Oh, how I wish you were still here with me and could see that I have changed. If you were...It is my prayer that you would forgive me."

He remained kneeling for quite some time. Before standing, he leaned over and kissed the tombstones under which his wife and son were interred, then spent a moment longer at the gravesites. Over the years since the accident, he'd asked Amanda for her forgiveness, but he never thought she was listening. As the wind whistled through the trees that day, Jacob got the feeling that she finally acknowledged his plea.

Chapter Thirteen

Jacob slung his knapsack over his shoulder and proceeded to the rail yard. He found a freight train bound for Baltimore and jumped aboard an empty boxcar, laying his head on his knapsack and bedding down for a nap.

The trip to Baltimore was uneventful until the train stopped in Pittsburgh. While in the yard, Jacob heard some men talking as they made their way down the rails toward his car. The door slid open, spilling sunlight into the boxcar. Jacob ducked back and hid in a dark corner. The men began erecting a makeshift ramp, failing to notice him. Moments later he heard the bellowing of livestock. One by one, the cattle walked up the ramp and into the boxcar, nine in all.

Just my luck—passengers, he quipped to himself. The door closed, cutting off the light, leaving Jacob alone and in the darkness with his fellow travelers. It wasn't long before the train whistle sounded, signaling that the next leg of Jacob's journey was about to begin. Not long out of the yard, he decided to resume his nap, which was interrupted shortly thereafter when he felt something warm and wet lapping at his cheek. Still half snoozing, he dreamed of a beautiful, fair maiden softly bathing his face with a wet cloth. What a pleasant feeling. His eyes eased open and adjusted to the dim light, causing him to recoil at the reality of his dream. There was no fair maiden, just a goofy-looking calf licking the side of his face. As he wiped the cow juice from his cheek with the sleeve of his coat, he couldn't help laughing. The little fella was as cute as could be. Jacob tried to gently shoo him away, but the calf just kept coming back. Eventually, it lay down next to him on a pile of hay.

"Moe... That's what I'll call you... little Moe," Jacob said as he petted the calf on the forehead. *Having company on the trip isn't as bad as I thought it was going to be.*

It wasn't fifteen minutes later when Jacob realized there was going to be a problem. Things were getting a bit unpleasant in the odor department. Cow flatulence. What came next was even worse. *So much for pleasant company.*

It took a while to become accustomed to the smell, but after some time it wasn't all that bad. The air was getting cold. Moe's thick fur cast off a wave of comforting heat, so Jacob edged over a little closer. Moe responded by washing Jacob's face again. He tried, unsuccessfully, to fend him off. Jacob and his friend kept each other warm for the remainder of the trip.

The train began to slow as it approached the Baltimore yard. Jacob stood. So did Moe. "This is where we part ways, little buddy. It's been nice traveling with you."

As the train stopped, Jacob jumped to the ground and began his walk into the city. His journey took him through the rough part of town. As he passed a neighborhood tavern, he came upon a group of three young men sitting on a bench outside the front door. He could tell they were drunk, so he crossed to the other side of the street. They crossed over, as well. Jacob knew what was coming next. He had been in similar situations before. Following his instincts, he took off running, but was no match for the fleet-footed young punks. They caught him and began to administer a beating. Jacob was able to get in a few good punches, but he was overpowered and outnumbered by the strapping young men, who robbed him of the small amount of money he carried.

Blood gushed from a cut on his head as he lay cursing the bullies who'd jumped him then run away like cowards. He picked himself up off the pavement and continued his walk. Blood ran down his forehead, staining his coat. He stopped to get a shirt from his backpack, balled it up, and held it against the cut on his head to stop the bleeding.

Jacob walked around the city for several hours searching for the address to the Salvation Army Mission. Finally he asked a stranger for directions and discovered that he was just a few blocks away from his destination.

Jacob arrived at the mission late that night. A middle-aged man with sandy blond hair, wearing a red and black checkered shirt, sat at the front desk.

"I'm here to see Pastor Bob Parsley."

"That would be me. How can I help you?"

"My name is Jacob McCallum. Howard Angel, in Chicago, sent me to see you."

"Oh, yes. I've been expecting you."

He stood to shake Jacob's hand.

"Wow, that's a nasty gash in your head. What happened?"

"I ran into the official greeting party a while ago. A bunch of thugs who took my money."

"You certainly got a good greeting. I'm very sorry about that."

"That's quite okay. I'll be fine."

"We need to get that cut looked at. Appears to me you could use a few stitches. Let's get you to the hospital."

"Nah, I'll be just fine. I've had a lot worse than this."

"All the same, you need to get that thing stitched up."

Bob called for a cab and accompanied Jacob to the emergency room. Upon arriving, an unsympathetic-looking heavy-set nurse handed him a form on a clipboard and Jacob filled out the required information. After completing the form, he took a seat in the waiting room. About thirty minutes later a pleasant-looking nurse came out to get him, taking him back to an empty room.

"You can sit here, sir. The doctor will be in momentarily."

Jacob took a seat, observing all the equipment in the room, curious as to its purpose.

"Hello, sir," the doctor said as he entered the room looking at Jacob's chart. "Let's see . . . you're Mr. McCallum. That's quite an ugly-looking cut you have there. It says here you were beaten by some strangers."

"Yeah, I got jumped by a group of young hooligans. There were three of them. In my day, I could have taken them all on."

"I'll bet you could have." The doctor smiled warmly. "I'm Dr. Brown. Mr. McCallum, we need to sew that gash up so it heals properly."

Dr. Brown dipped a square of gauze into a container and began cleaning Jacob's wound with some disinfectant, causing him to pull back in discomfort. Jacob watched, apprehensively, as the doctor retrieved a needle and some sutures from the table and brought the needle toward the cut on his head.

"This is going to sting a little," Dr. Brown warned.

"Ouch! It sure does."

"Are you from here in Baltimore?"

"No. I just got in from Chicago."

"What brings you here?"

"Ouch! That hurts!"

"Sorry."

"It's a rather long and involved story, but I'm here to find my daughter."

"Find her?"

"Yes, we've been estranged for about seven or eight years. My wish is to find her and make things right. Ouch!" Jacob winced again.

"Well, I'm finished here. I wish you luck in finding your daughter."

"Thank you, Dr. Brown."

On the cab ride back to the Salvation Army Mission, Jacob and Bob Parsley became better acquainted.

"Howard Angel is a good friend of mine. We went to school together."

"Yeah, he's a real nice guy. He helped me out a lot."

"Howard told me you were going through some tough times. He seems to have a real fondness for you."

"We became pretty good friends while I stayed at his mission in Chicago."

"He told me you've come a long way...stopped drinking and smoking and even renewed your faith."

"It wasn't easy, none of it. Kicking my drinking and smoking habits was the easiest part. Renewing my faith was a bit more difficult. I didn't ever think I would find my faith again, and I worry daily about losing it."

"That happens to all of us from time to time. The important thing is keeping faith in your heart."

"There's where I have trouble. Things happen in my life and I lose faith. Howard was good at reminding me that faith is imperative. I'll need a lot of it to find my daughter and make peace with her."

Pastor Bob let Jacob sleep in his room that night, offering Jacob the opportunity for some privacy and the prospect of a good night's rest.

* * *

Jacob woke up the next morning with a terrible headache. He reached up and felt the large knot on the top of his head, recalling the incident that was to blame for all of this.

"Darn, that hurts."

Sitting up in bed, Jacob took in his surroundings. As he attempted to rise, the pain in his head intensified, causing him to sit back down on the edge of the bed. Pastor Bob poked his head in the door and greeted him.

"How'd you sleep last night?"

"Pretty good, but it felt much better going to sleep than waking up." Jacob pointed to his bandaged head.

"How is your head this morning?"

"Pounding like a drum."

"I'll bet it is. You took a good thumping yesterday. Want some coffee?"

"You don't know how bad I need a cup of coffee right now."

"Come and join me in the dining hall. We'll get you some coffee and I'll introduce you to some of the guys."

Jacob followed Pastor Bob to a table where a group of men were seated.

"Good morning, Bob," shouted a man at the table.

"Good morning, John. I'd like to introduce you all to a friend of mine. This is Jacob McCallum. He joined us last night. Came all the way from Chicago."

"Nice to meet you," John said as he got up from his chair to shake Jacob's hand. "This is Mitch and Bill. Those two over there are Jim and Steven." John pointed.

"Nice to meet all of you."

"Have a seat."

Bob and Jacob sat down with the group.

"These gentlemen head up our bell ringing committee."

"Bell ringing committee?"

"Yes. You have heard of the Salvation Army Bell Ringers, haven't you? They ring Christmas bells on the street corners during the holiday season to raise money for our mission."

"We can always use extra bell ringers, Jacob. Are you interested in joining us?" John asked.

"Well...that's something I need to think about."

"I've been doing it for three years," Jim boasted. "It really gets you into the spirit of Christmas."

"Let me know as soon as you can. We're organizing the bell ringing project next week," John told him.

"I'll think about it and let you know. But I'm here to find my daughter. That's the most important thing to me right now."

Jacob and Bob remained at the table and ate breakfast with the group.

* * *

Sitting at the kitchen table, Dr. Nathaniel Brown read the morning newspaper. His wife placed a plate of steaming scrambled eggs and dark toast in front of him. Taking a sip of his coffee, he said, "I met an interesting gentleman last night at the hospital."

"Oh, really?"

"Pastor Bob brought him in. He had just arrived in Baltimore and was jumped by a gang of young men who put a nasty gash on his head."

"That's terrible. What was so interesting about him?"

"I don't know. He just seemed like a very nice old fellow who has lost his way. He said he was here to locate his daughter. They've been estranged for years."

"Ah, that's so sad. Why are they estranged?"

"He didn't say. But it is sad, indeed."

Chapter Fourteen

By now, Jacob had settled in comfortably at the mission. He made new friends and was becoming involved in the mission's resources to help him stay on the straight and narrow. He even joined the Alcoholics Anonymous group. Jacob quickly realized why Howard Angel spoke so highly of Bob Parsley. In his short time at the mission, he and Pastor Bob struck up a close relationship. Jacob relished the camaraderie and felt as though he was part of something good. His journey of faith continued to flourish, too.

One evening while sitting on his cot, Jacob started a conversation with Frankie. "Frankie...I wish you could see me now. I think you'd be proud of your ol' papa. I'm so sorry for all the things that I did and for how my life turned out, and yours. I know you are looking down on me and that you can see the changes I have made in my life. I also believe that you have forgiven me, as has your mom."

Truth was, Jacob was extremely proud of himself. Still troubled by his less than successful reunion with Tom, it was with renewed hope that he would begin his search for Emma. Coming to terms with the fact that he could do nothing about his past, he considered the future with more optimistic prospects.

Pastor Bob quietly opened the door to check in on Jacob. Seeing him in conversation with Frankie, he paused at the door and listened.

"I'm proud of you, son. You died a hero fighting for your country. I'm sure your mom is proud of you, too. Give her a big hug and kiss for me, will you?"

Sensing Jacob was through, Bob made his entrance. As he walked down the row of cots in the room, he called: "Jacob?"

"Oh, hi, Bob."

"Sorry for intruding. Can I join you?"

"Sure, have a seat."

Bob took a seat on the cot across from Jacob.

"I've been sitting here for hours. Just got finished praying and having a little talk with Frankie. I think I finally get it."

"Get what?"

"All the things Howard told me. At least some of them. I didn't understand at the time, but once he said, "It's one of the greatest gifts you can give yourself, to forgive. Forgive everybody, *including yourself*." Finally, I have managed to do just that…forgive myself."

"Forgiveness comes from those who are strong, Jacob. It is the weak who seem to have difficulty with forgiveness."

"That makes sense to me now. It just came to me when I was sitting here talking to Frankie."

Jacob's mouth opened with a broad smile, and the deep creases on his forehead gave way to cheerful wrinkles at the sides of his eyes, accentuating his grin. And though the twinkle in his eyes was from tears, they were happy tears.

Bob leaned toward Jacob and firmly patted him on the leg. "Why don't you come out and join us in the dining hall. John's playing the guitar and all the guys are gathered around singing some old songs. We could use another strong voice."

"Mine's strong…just a little off-key, that's all."

They sang until late into the night…old folk songs, hymns, and they even tried out some favorite Christmas tunes to practice for the approaching holiday before turning in.

Jacob laughed with his friends as they ate their morning meal. He was finally fitting in. After breakfast he began his morning chores around the mission. As he mopped the floor, he couldn't stop thinking about Emma. *Where is she? Is she still here in Baltimore?* He felt a deep yearning to find her. As he plunged the mop into a pail of water, he came to the undeniable conclusion that his desire to find his daughter was overpowering his ability to do anything else. Leaning the wet mop against the wall, he abandoned his task and went in search of Bob.

Knocking on Bob's office door, he entered without even waiting for a response. Bob was working at his desk, shuffling through some papers. The intrusion caught him off guard, startling him a little.

"Pastor Bob!"

"What is it, Jacob?"

"I need to go and try to find Emma."

Bob looked somewhat surprised. "Now?"

"Yes. Today. Just as soon as I can. Will you help me?"

"Do you think you're ready to make this journey?"

"Yes. I'm sure."

"Well…let me finish up here. Come back in about fifteen minutes and we'll make a plan."

Jacob grinned widely. The expression on his face told Bob that it was time...time to help his friend accomplish his goal and the final leg of his voyage for forgiveness. Jacob turned and cheerfully walked out the door.

"Jacob, wait!"

He poked his head back through the doorway, eyebrows raised.

"I can do this paperwork later. Let's get started. Come on back in and sit down."

Jacob took a seat in front of Bob's desk, where they devised a strategy. Then they headed to the courthouse, where they began their search. They plowed through volumes of city directories and tax records, looking through dozens of books. "There sure are a lot of Browns here," Jacob observed.

Bob laughed. "Be thankful her name's not Smith."

After a few hours, Jacob, his eyes strained, looked up at Bob and said with disappointment, "Well, Bob—no luck here. Looks like we came up empty."

"That's all right. We just need to move on and look elsewhere."

Next they went from church to church, checking the registers to see if she was a member.

"Emma Brown...that doesn't ring a bell." They heard that repeated a number of times throughout the day. Running out of places to search, they resorted to asking strangers on the street if they knew of her. Their search was futile.

The day ended much less optimistically than it had begun, and Jacob was far less enthusiastic at dinner. Unusually quiet, he sat staring down at his plate while he ate.

"Any luck finding your daughter today?" John asked.

Jacob didn't answer right away, keeping his attention focused on his plate. "No."

"Nothing?"

"No. Pastor Bob and I spent the day trying, but we couldn't find even find the slightest sign that she lives here."

"Are you going to look for her again tomorrow?"

Jacob deferred to Pastor Bob, who nodded. "Yeah. We're going to give it another try tomorrow, aren't we, Jacob?"

"I'll search until I find her. That's why I came here."

"I'll be right there with you," Pastor Bob reassured him.

"She'll turn up. I know she will," John said optimistically.

Jacob's head bobbled with skepticism.

"Cheer up, Baltimore's a big place. I'm sure we'll have better luck tomorrow," Bob assured him.

The following day, their search resumed. All day they labored to find just a small trace of evidence that could lead them to Emma. But their efforts were met with the same results as the day before. Their search went on for several more days with no favorable outcome, not even a clue.

"I don't think I'll ever find her, Bob," Jacob said out of frustration.

"Keep the faith."

"My faith is stretched to its limit. Maybe it's time for me to move on. I don't know where else to look. I'm beginning to think that coming here to Baltimore was a waste of time."

"How can you say that? Has our friendship been a waste of time? Have your friendships with the others here at the mission been a waste of time? How about the enrichment of your faith, has that been a waste of time? Come on, Jacob!"

"I didn't mean it that way. I meant that my search for Emma has been a waste of time."

"Maybe it's time to give it a rest, just for a while. This is going to take some time."

"It's all I can think about, finding Emma."

"Maybe you need something to take your mind off of it."

"Like what?"

"Have you given any thought about what John asked?"

"What do you mean?"

"About becoming a bell ringer?"

"Not really."

"Well?"

"I don't think it's right for me. I'd feel awkward—ringing a bell on the street corner."

"Awkward?"

"I don't feel all that comfortable around people anymore, especially in that setting."

"Come on, Jacob. This is a chance for you to draw on your old skills. Surely if you were so successful selling railroad equipment, you can sell people on the idea of giving to help others, especially at Christmastime. You're always saying how you have thrown your life away. Here's a chance for you to get some of it back."

"I don't know..."

"Jacob, you say you want forgiveness and redemption. This would put you on the path to those things. This is one way you can give back some of what you have taken. Do it, Jacob."

"I just don't know if I can."

"Sure you can. We'll all be behind you. This is an opportunity for you to do some real good."

Jacob thought for a moment. "You're right! I guess it wouldn't be all that bad."

"Of course it wouldn't. You'll have our support. Please, Jacob."

After thoughtful consideration, Jacob replied. "All right, I'll give it a try. But I can't guarantee how successful I'll be."

"I have no doubt you'll be successful," Bob said warmly.

* * *

It was the day after Thanksgiving, the day the Salvation Army bells would begin to ring around the world. Excited, yet apprehensive, Jacob looked forward to his new job. The plans called for him to man the corner of Charles and Light Streets, a very busy intersection in the center of town near fancy shops and businesses. At first it felt strange to him as he timidly rang the bell. Passersby were stingy. For the first half of the day, the only money in the kettle was put there by Jacob himself. It amounted to half of all he had. Feeling guilty, he emptied the remaining money from his pocket and threw it in the pot. He was embarrassed to take the paltry contents of his kettle back to the mission.

"How'd you fare today, Jacob?" Bob asked.

"Not so well. Maybe I'm not cut out for this."

"Have patience. I'm confident you'll use your ingenuity to find a way to be successful. Remember, this is your chance to give back."

The next day was bitter cold; snow flurries filled the air. Jacob shivered as he rang the bell, this day with more enthusiasm. Despite his renewed efforts, he felt invisible. There was so much activity, yet very few givers. He became angry and began ringing the bell as loud as he could. Still, few people dropped money into his kettle. Frustrated, he began asking people to give in the "Spirit of Christmas." This approach was met with some success, but still fell short of his expectations. Again, he returned to the mission with a mere pittance.

That night, Jacob sought refuge in the chapel. There, he prayed and thought about his situation, having difficulty reconciling all the changes he'd made in his life against his failure to find Emma and his miserable failure as a bell ringer. What else could he do? He'd stopped drinking and smoking. He'd forgiven himself for his past transgressions. He had become a man of faith, yet still, he was miserable. He was desperate to make a difference in the world, determined to open people's hearts to giving, but it was such a struggle.

The back door to the chapel opened and Bob walked up to him.

"I've been looking for you. Thought I might find you here."

"Bob, I'm so disappointed. I thought this would be a way for me to make up for some of the bad things I've done in my life. It's just not working out. I don't know what else to do."

"I know you've asked for forgiveness. You *are* forgiven. You told me you even forgave yourself. Have faith. You'll find a way. You're doing good things here. And if you can't find Emma, at least you tried. That's all you can do."

"But I want to do more than just try."

"We all appreciate your efforts. You'll find a way to make it work. I know you will. Just keep praying on it."

The following morning, Jacob took to the streets once more, giving it his best effort, trying to be more cheerful…more approachable. As the day wore on, he thankfully received the generosity of more people as they merrily dropped coins into his kettle.

"Merry Christmas, sir," Jacob thanked a giver.

"Thank you, ma'am," he said to another.

The day was going well. Jacob's kettle was heavy with offerings when he carried it back to the mission.

"Ho-ho-ho!" he shouted as he burst through the front door. Beaming with pride and joy, he emptied the contents of his kettle onto the table to be counted.

"Hey, Jacob," Bob said.

"I had an incredible day. Just look at all the money from my kettle!"

"See, I told you that you'd be successful," Bob said.

After all the kettles were tallied, Jacob had collected the most. Before going to bed, he visited the chapel to give thanks. His prayers had been answered.

After his prayer time, Jacob began cleaning out a closet at the mission for Bob. While rummaging around in some old boxes, he discovered an old Santa's hat and coat. He took them out of the box and put them on for fun.

"Hey, guys...look at me. I'm Santa Claus."

"You sure are a skinny Santa." John laughed as did several other of his friends.

"Yeah, but I sure am jolly. Ho-ho-ho!"

Bob heard the clamor and came to investigate. Seeing Jacob, he couldn't help joining in the laughter.

"I'm going to wear this tomorrow while I ring the bell and I'll put you all to shame when we count the money."

"If you want to look like a fool, go ahead," one of his friends kidded.

"I'll be happy to look like a fool if I can fill my kettle with donations."

This moment of levity seemed to give Jacob a boost of confidence. He took the hat and coat and placed them under his cot before climbing on and going to sleep.

After breakfast, Jacob dressed in his Santa suit, leaving the mission with his bell in hand, his kettle tucked securely under his arm. With a robust feeling of determination, he stood on the street corner and clowned with the passersby, wishing them a Merry Christmas and asking them to reach deep into their pockets to fill the kettle with change. His presence made people laugh, and they gave freely. Some even opened their billfolds and gave folding money. He was having the time of his life. The more people gave, the more cheerful Jacob became. The more cheerful he became, the more they gave.

Again, Jacob had collected more than any of the other bell ringers. As he did every night, he visited the chapel to give thanks before going to bed. So ecstatic about his performance over the past few days, he could hardly contain himself on the way to his cot. He passed Bob on the way.

"Congratulations, Jacob. I heard how well you did again today."

"I don't think I have ever been this happy, not in years anyway. It feels so good."

"You should be proud. We're all proud of you. You're playing a big role in our success this year."

"Bob, I feel free. I am done dwelling on my past. I care about the present, and what the future holds. For the first time in years, the present isn't so bad."

"Alleluia."

"Though I am very ashamed of my past, I can't go back and change any of it—or I would. I can only go forward. I realize forgiveness is a gift that can't be demanded, only requested through prayer and grace. I don't care what others think anymore. For the first time in a long while, I feel at peace with myself."

"That's fantastic. I'm so happy for you."

"Bob, I have a huge favor to ask you."

"Anything, Jacob."

"We've become close friends. The only true friends I have in my life are you and Howard Angel. You have both been so good to me...and you led me to the trough."

Bob looked at him quizzically.

"I want to be baptized. I want you to be the one to do it. Bathe me in the water of baptism so I can begin my new life."

"Certainly, it would be my honor."

Bob prayed with Jacob. Overwhelmed, Jacob wept openly as he embraced Bob.

"When would you like to be baptized?"

"The sooner the better. How about tomorrow?"

"Tomorrow?" Bob said with surprise. "Consider it done, Jacob. You've made me so very proud."

After their conversation, Bob felt compelled to share the good news with Howard Angel, since it was he who had planted the seeds that led Jacob to this moment. He called Howard in Chicago.

"That's wonderful, Bob," Howard said. "Has Jacob found Emma yet?"

"We've looked, but haven't found any sign of her. Sadly, I wonder if she is even here. It's been years since he saw her last. She could be anywhere."

"That's too bad. The poor man needs a break. I know finding her and having her give him forgiveness would go a long way to restoring his soul. Tell Jacob I wish I could be there for his baptism. Give him my best."

"You know I will, Howard."

★ ★ ★

The next day was glorious. The sunshine sparkled through the stained glass windows, filling the room with fractured rays of colored lights. Bob prepared the chapel for this wonderful occasion and told all the mission's residents of the blessed event. The room was full as Jacob took his place in the front of the chapel.

Dressed in long white robes, he and Bob stood ready. There was a small pool filled with water behind the altar, but high on the stage so everyone could see. Bob was first to enter the pool. He nodded, signaling Jacob that it was time. Jacob tested the water. It was cold. He pulled his foot back out, causing laughter in the church. Bob laughed, too.

"Come on in, Jacob. The water's fine." He smiled.

Jacob slid over the edge and waded over to where Bob awaited him. They smiled at each other, then Bob gave Jacob a nod, letting him know the ceremony was about to begin. Jacob took his position in front of Bob, crossing his arms and pulling them close to his chest, surrendering himself. Pastor Bob gently laid his hands on Jacob's shoulders and submerged him in the sacred water. From beneath the pool, Jacob stared up at Bob, his eyes wide open. Looking down at him, Bob observed a humorous grin on Jacob's face. He fought his impulse to laugh at Jacob's childlike enthusiasm. When he emerged from the water, born again, the chapel erupted in applause. It was done. Jacob was truly on his way to redemption.

Chapter Fifteen

Jacob's success as a bell ringer continued. His cheerful demeanor caught on among the people of Baltimore. Many of the same people gave every day. The word circulated around town about this nice, entertaining gentleman who was doing such good work. He made giving fun. Some walked long distances, past other Salvation Army helpers, to place money in Jacob's kettle...pennies, nickels, dimes, and quarters. Every now and then someone would place dollar bills into his kettle. Incredibly, people waited in long lines to give their money to Jacob. His success as a bell ringer became legendary. The money he raised was helping many of the less fortunate in town. As his notoriety grew, *The Baltimore Sun* newspaper wrote an article about him: THE CHEERFUL BELL RINGER, the headline read. The article was long, and very favorable to Jacob. His emerging fame resulted in more generous offerings as he rang the bell. There was a lot of buzz about Jacob on the streets and in the churches, where much of the money he raised was donated for hunger programs. Indeed, things were going well.

Dr. Brown sipped his morning coffee while reading the newspaper. He came upon the article about Jacob and read it with interest.

"That's the man I treated at the hospital."

"What?" his wife said.

"The old man I treated for the cut on his head a while back... There's an article about him and a photo in the newspaper."

"Oh, I remember you saying something about him. What did he do?"

"He didn't do anything, what I mean is, he didn't do anything wrong... quite the opposite. He's been ringing the bell for the Salvation Army and apparently has become somewhat of a celebrity. It says here, people are lining up just to put money in his kettle."

"That's nice, dear. You said there was something interesting about him."

Dr. Brown finished his breakfast and went off to the hospital. His wife cleaned up the dishes. She picked up the newspaper from the table and, without looking at it, threw it in the trash.

★ ★ ★

It was a cold and snowy afternoon. Jacob was merrily ringing his bell dressed in his Santa suit when he noticed a little girl, about ten years old, staring at him from across the street. She stood there for the longest time, just watching him. *Is he the real Santa?* she wondered. He stopped for a moment and looked over at her, not able to figure out her interest in him. Resuming the ringing of his bell, he joyfully greeted everyone on the busy street corner as they dropped money into his kettle. The girl continued to watch as people gave unselfishly. The sight brought a beaming smile to her face. The next time Jacob looked across the street, she was gone—just as quietly and mysteriously as she'd appeared.

As evening approached, Jacob returned to the mission juggling his kettle and several bags of coins. When he laid his bounty on the table, he got an ovation from his friends. This lifted Jacob's spirits even higher. After talking and joking around with his fellow bell ringers, as was his habit, he retreated to the chapel to give thanks and to pray before being joined by Bob Parsley.

"Jacob, you are doing such great work. We have never had a more successful season."

"Oh, collecting the money has become easy for me. I'm a very lucky man."

"It's not only the collections I'm talking about. It's your complete transformation. I've been in touch with Howard and he said to tell you how proud of you he is, as well."

"Thank you. But I wouldn't say I have made a *complete* transformation just yet. I still have much to learn, much to do, and a ton of bad things I have done in the past to make up for."

"You certainly are off to an abundant start."

"Could I ask for another favor?"

Laughing, Bob said, "Don't tell me you want to get baptized again!"

Looking at him with a grin, Jacob said, "No. Not that. I'd like to use the telephone to call Howard."

"No problem. I'll take you to my office and dial his number for you."

"Thank you so much."

As Bob dialed up Howard, Jacob felt butterflies in his stomach in anticipation of speaking with his old friend. The phone began to ring and Bob handed it to Jacob.

"Hello. You reached the Salvation Army. This is Howard Angel. Can I help you?"

"Howard, it's Jacob."

"Jacob, what a pleasant surprise! It's so good to hear your voice."

"You have no idea how good it is to hear yours."

"Bob told me how well you've adjusted, and all the wonderful things you've been doing. He even sent me the article from *The Baltimore Sun*. You're becoming quite a celebrity there in Baltimore."

"You had a lot to do with all of this, you know."

"Nah, you've been blessed and it has nothing to do with me. You're the one who needs to be commended."

"You put me on the path to righteousness. I've never been happier. I'm so grateful you pulled me out of the alley that day and took me under your wing."

"Isn't that what angels are supposed to do?"

They both laughed.

"It's good to hear you haven't lost your sense of humor. How are things going for you out there in Chicago?"

"Everything out here is good, except we all miss you."

"I miss you, too. Tell everyone I said hello."

"Will do. Bob tells me that you've been searching for Emma but haven't found her yet."

"No. I've been so busy ringing the bell that I haven't had much time to look for her lately. I ask just about everyone I see if they know her—nothing yet. Right now, I'm content with my job ringing the bell and collecting for the poor."

"I hope you find her, and I hope she embraces you with an open heart."

"I don't know about that, but I'll give it my best try right after Christmas. The rest is up to her. It's out of my hands."

"I wish you the best. I have a feeling everything is going to turn out good for you. You certainly deserve it."

"Thank you, Howard. I guess I should hang up now. I don't want to run up the telephone bill since Bob was generous enough to let me use the phone to call you. Merry Christmas."

"Okay, Jacob. It's been wonderful talking with you. Merry Christmas... and good-bye."

"Good-bye, Howard."

★ ★ ★

That night, the little girl who had been watching Jacob ring his bell earlier in the day helped her mother wash and dry the dishes. Unusually quiet, she had something important weighing on her mind.

"Mommy?"

"Yes, dear?"

"You know the money I have been saving?"

"Yes?"

"I saw a man dressed like Santa today ringing a bell and collecting money for the Salvation Army."

"And?"

"He looks like a nice man, and I want to know if I can put the money I saved in his kettle."

"I wonder if that is the man your daddy was reading about in the newspaper."

"What?"

"Oh, nothing. Are you sure you want to use your money that way?"

"It's to help poor people."

"I know, but you've been saving for a long time."

"Yes. I've been saving up for a new doll. But my old doll is just fine. I'd kinda like to give my money to the poor so they have a nice Christmas."

"If that's what you want to do, it would be very generous of you."

"Can I do it tomorrow?"

"I don't see why not."

★ ★ ★

Jacob dreamed deeply that night. In his dream, Jacob met a woman who said she knew Emma, and she gave Jacob her address. Delighted at learning of Emma's whereabouts, Jacob's hopes were rallied. Finally, he would have the opportunity to get reacquainted with his daughter and hopefully to gain her forgiveness. He set out immediately for the address the woman had given him. When he arrived at Emma's address, he became overwhelmed with emotion. His stomach churned with anxiety. While walking up the few steps to the front door, his knees buckled. Pausing at the door, he took a deep breath before knocking.

Emma came to the door. Opening it, she got the surprise of her life when she saw her father standing there. She began to cry and embraced him. They stood there for a moment in each other's arms without saying a word. Then she spoke. "Dad, I never thought I'd see you again. Where have you been? I'm so happy to see you."

She kissed him on the cheek.

"Well, don't just stand there, come on in!" Emma pulled him through the doorway by the hand.

"Emma, I came to apologize for all I have done and to ask your forgiveness."

"Oh, Dad, I forgive you. I do. I've missed you so much."

Astonished, Jacob said, "You do?"

"Yes. I wish our last meeting hadn't ended so abruptly. I should have given you a chance. I'm sorry."

"That's all right, my dear. We're together again now. Let's make the best of it."

Suddenly a young girl appeared in the room.

"This is your grandpa. Come over here and give him a big hug."

Jacob kneeled down on one knee and opened his arms. The little girl ran over and enthusiastically hugged him. Jacob smiled broadly.

The touching scene was interrupted by the ringing of Jacob's alarm clock, startling him awake. The smile faded from his face as he realized the wonderful reunion was just a dream. He closed his eyes in hopes of recapturing the moment with Emma and his granddaughter, but it was gone—faded away. Devastated it was but a dream, though a pleasant one, Jacob sat up on the edge of his bed and rubbed his face, a bit bewildered, as he thought about Emma. His brief moment of joy was replaced by sadness and the yearning to reconnect with her. The dream made him want to search for her again, but he didn't even know where to begin. He and Bob had already been down that road and it was a dead end.

Before going to breakfast, he went into the bathroom to splash the sleep from his face. The cool water revitalized him. He stared at his reflection in the mirror for a moment, wondering if he would ever see Emma again. Then, he toweled off his face and went out to eat his morning meal.

After breakfast and sharing some laughs with his buddies, Jacob trudged through the snow-covered sidewalks to get to the corner of Charles and Light. He arrived a bit early. After setting up his kettle, he sat on a stoop at the entrance to a building.

"Good morning, Jacob. I brought you some coffee to warm you up."

The woman who owned the restaurant next to where Jacob rang his bell handed him the cup of hot coffee.

"Thank you, Mabel. It looks like it's going to be a cold one today."

"If you need more coffee, or need to get warm, stop in and visit with us for a while."

"Will do."

Jacob took his gloves off and cupped the coffee mug in his hands. The warm coffee was a welcome relief to the cold that stung his hands. As he sat there, even before ringing his bell for the first time, people began filling his kettle with their generosity. Feeling he should begin ringing the bell, Jacob set down his coffee, which wafted steam into the frigid air. After putting on his gloves, he retrieved his bell and prepared to ring it. He pulled the bell back over his shoulder then shook it in his hand, anticipating its ring. His motion produced nothing but silence.

He shook it again, harder—still nothing. At a loss, he looked into the bell and discovered the clapper was frozen solid to the side of it. After freeing the clapper, he chuckled to himself, then began ringing merrily as the sound of his bell carried for blocks.

As Jacob looked around for donors, he noticed the little girl he'd seen the day before standing across the street. Again, she just stood there looking at him. When he glanced back at her, she turned her head as if she was standing there for some other purpose. They stared at each other numerous times. When their eyes met, she would again look away. This went on for about ten minutes.

Suddenly she garnered the courage to approach him, stepping off the curb after looking up and down the street for approaching traffic. She crossed over to Jacob's side, walking up to him with a somewhat timid expression. When she arrived at the kettle, she stood there continuing to observe Jacob collecting money before looking up at him, her bright blue eyes blinking several times.

They stood silent, staring at each other before Jacob, in a reassuring tone, said, "What is it, honey?"

"Good morning, sir," she said.

"Good morning."

She was standing there with a jar full of change.

"Sir, I have been saving my money for a long time. Can I put it in your kettle?"

"Are you sure that's what you want to do? There are a lot of coins in that jar."

"Oh, yes. I'm real sure."

Jacob tilted the kettle in her direction as she spilled the contents of the jar into it. The coins made the most beautiful sound as they hit the bottom. The generous offering from someone so young and innocent made the sound even more gratifying.

"Thank you so very much. Merry Christmas and may God bless you."

She stood there and kept looking at him. His Santa coat and hat along with his white beard made him resemble Saint Nick.

"What is it?" he asked gently.

"Are you Santa?"

Jacob laughed. "No. I'm just one of his helpers."

She continued gazing at him.

"What's your name?" he asked.

"Mary."

"That's a pretty name."

Jacob stared off into space for a brief moment. Mary was his granddaughter's name. Thinking about her made him sad.

"What's wrong, mister?"

"Oh, nothing. You just reminded me of someone there for a moment."

"What's your name?"

Jacob thought for an instant then playfully said, "You can call me 'Jingles' if you want to. That's what Santa calls me. Do you live nearby?"

"Not far from here. Just down the street. Where do you live?"

"Well, actually, I don't have a home. You see, I'm poor and I live at the Salvation Army Mission. It's a great place to live."

"Can I ring the bell once?"

"Sure you can."

He handed the bell to Mary. She gripped it quite awkwardly and began ringing it shyly.

"Oh, come on, you can do better than that. You need to ring it loud to get people's attention. Here, let me show you."

Jacob positioned himself behind her. Grasping her right arm, he moved it up and down, demonstrating the proper technique. She got the hang of it real quick.

"That's it. You're going great!"

Mary's face radiated a deep sense of pride. When she received her first donation, she looked up at Jacob and smiled. He winked at her, nodding his head. This motivated her to ring the bell even louder. All but a few passersby dropped coins into the bucket. The gifts were pouring in as Mary delighted in ringing the bell. After a short while she began to slow down. It was obvious that she was tiring.

"Jingles, my arm is getting tired. Can you ring it for a while?"

Jacob laughed. "You had me scared a little bit. You were doing so well I was afraid you were going to put me out of a job."

"Whew, I don't know how you can do this all day without your arm getting sore."

"It's not my arm as much as it is my aching back," he said, grinning. "Why don't you stand next to the kettle and tell people Merry Christmas as they walk by?"

"Okay."

She positioned herself beside the kettle and greeted everyone she saw.

"You're doing great," Jacob encouraged her.

"You give all this money to poor people?"

"I am doing this for the Salvation Army. They give the money to the poor."

"Oh."

"Actually, it's the generosity of all these people who make it possible to help others."

"A few people didn't even look at me when I was ringing the bell. They just walked by without putting any money in the kettle."

"Well, some people may not have much money and can't afford to give. Others may not be moved by the spirit of giving and wish to keep their money for themselves."

"That's being stingy."

"Yes, but God doesn't want people to give if they don't give freely. He loves those who give without reservation. The small gifts from those with little are more valuable to God than the gifts from the rich."

"Wow, I didn't know that."

Jacob resumed ringing the bell. Large fluffy snowflakes began to fall, and a group of carolers started singing on the opposite street corner. The ringing bell, the snow, the carolers...the mood was perfect for inspiring the Christmas spirit in the hearts of everyone around. People flocked to Jacob's kettle to give.

Mary and Jacob had a wonderful time. They talked and laughed. She relieved Jacob from time to time so he could rest his arm...and his back. As the day wore on, Jacob suggested that Mary go home so her parents wouldn't worry about her.

"Will I see you tomorrow?" he asked.

Mary thought for a moment. She couldn't think of anything else she'd rather be doing during her Christmas vacation from school.

"If Mommy lets me come up here again."

"I hope she does. I could sure use your help."

What he meant was...he would sure enjoy her company.

"Bye, Mr. Jingles."

Mary skipped down the street, giving Jacob one last look over her shoulder before she turned the corner and disappeared from his sight.

By the day's end, Jacob could hardly carry the kettle back to the mission. The money raised by Jacob thus far amounted to more than what was collected by all the other bell ringers combined. His tally alone far surpassed the prior year's total for the entire campaign.

"How do you do it, Jacob?" John asked while counting out the money Jacob dumped on the table.

"First of all, I love what I do. The generous people of Baltimore are responsible for the rest. The glory goes to them and to God."

Bob overheard the conversation and smiled.

Jacob's thoughts kept returning to Emma. He was optimistic that time would facilitate their reunion. However, for now, he stayed focused on his mission to collect as much money as he could to help those in need, recognizing this was his calling for the moment. Ringing the bell filled his heart with the spirit of the holiday season. The significance of Christmas this year gave Jacob far more joy than it had in decades. But he couldn't shake the nagging vision of finding Emma. Doing so before the holiday would make it all the more spectacular.

Pastor Bob thumbed through some papers on his desk while entering the proceeds from the bell ringing campaign into his ledger. When he noticed the numbers that Jacob was posting, the wrinkles on his forehead became more prominent as he concentrated more closely. It was amazing. For a man who doubted himself so fiercely, Jacob was certainly outshining all the other bell ringers and far surpassing everyone's expectations, even those of Jacob himself.

Later that evening, Bob said, "I was in my office doing some paperwork. All this money you are collecting is giving me paperwork nightmares." Bob laughed.

"Ah, quit complaining," Jacob jested. "It gives you something to do and it keeps you out of trouble."

"Yeah, right," Bob joked.

"I met a little girl today while ringing my bell."

"That's nice."

"She's a special child, generous beyond her years."

"Yeah? Tell me about her."

"She walked up to me and poured a jar of coins she had been saving for a long time into my kettle."

Jacob's voice began to quiver, his eyes moistened. "She was so thoughtful and kind. It was the cutest thing. She actually thought I was Santa Claus." Jacob laughed.

"You are kind of convincing." Bob chuckled.

They looked at each other. From Jacob's expression, Bob could see that he was deeply touched.

"Perhaps she was a special blessing sent as a reward for your good deeds."

Jacob smiled while continuing to tell Bob more about her and the wonderful day they'd spent together.

Chapter Sixteen

Some of the other bell ringers viewed their repetitive task as mundane—just a job. Jacob found it invigorating. Keen on getting each day started, he got such hope and purpose from the simple act of ringing a bell. As Jacob set up his kettle, his emotions ran deep. A lump formed in the back of his throat and his eyes welled with joy. He looked to the sky, thanking his maker for another opportunity to initiate a positive difference in the world, and to pay back, if even in a small way, the good fortunes he once experienced—not to mention to repay what he stole while in his alcohol- and greed-infused state of mind.

The gray sky threatened more snow. Jacob inhaled the crisp morning air deeply into his lungs, waking his whole body.

After about an hour of ringing, he looked across the street, hoping to see Mary again. To his delight, there she stood, her face illuminated with a brilliant smile.

"Well, hello, Mary," he called to her from across the street.

"Hello, Mr. Jingles."

"Come on over here, but watch for traffic."

She ran across the street, almost breathless when she reached him.

"I told my mommy all about you. She said I could help you again today. She told me to tell you that you are doing wonderful things and to keep up the good work. Can I help you collect money again today?"

"Sure."

"I brought this coffee can from home. I can collect money in it."

Mary stood with Jacob the rest of the morning, collecting donations and putting them in his kettle. Her companionship made him feel content. They laughed and joked to pass the time. Oh, how he wished he hadn't thrown away his chance to have a relationship with Emma and his own granddaughter. He truly enjoyed Mary's company and felt blessed to have it.

"I'm going to go up the street and collect some money for you," Mary said a while later.

"Be careful."

"I will."

About an hour later she returned, her tin can overflowing.

"Great job, Mary," Jacob said with a big grin.

"I told a lot of people what you taught me about giving. They gave me lots of money," she said as she poured the money into the kettle.

"You hungry?"

"I sure am, Mr. Jingles."

"How about a hot dog?"

"That would be great!"

Jacob took Mary's hand and they walked into the restaurant next door to his kettle.

Mabel greeted them both with a smile.

"Come in and warm yourselves up for a bit. Who's your pretty friend, Jacob?"

"This is Mary. She's my helper."

"Well, hello, Mary."

"Hi, ma'am."

"Aren't you a pretty little girl?"

"Thank you."

"We're starved, Mabel. How about fixing us up with two of your delicious hot dogs? I'll have mine with mustard. How about you, Mary, what will you have on yours?"

"I'll have mustard, too."

"Okay, that's two dogs with mustards. Anything else?"

Jacob looked down at Mary, then back to Mabel and said, "Give us two hot chocolates with that, will you, Mabel?"

"Sure thing. Coming right up. Go sit at the table by the window and I'll bring everything out to you in a couple of minutes."

They took a seat by the window. As they looked out the window, they saw a woman and her child toss some money into Jacob's kettle.

"Look at that. They're giving generously and we're not even ringing the bell."

Mary pressed her nose against the window for a better look. "That was very nice."

"It sure was."

Mabel balanced a tray as she carried their food to the table. "Here you go, two dogs with mustard and two hot chocolates."

"I'm so hungry I could eat a cow," Jacob joked.

Mary laughed. "Me, too."

They talked while they ate...getting to know each other a little better as they shared tidbits about their lives.

"What do you want Santa to bring you?"

"Oh, I don't know. I'd like a new doll. That's what I was saving my money for."

"You put the money you were saving for a new doll into the kettle?"

"Yep."

"That was a magnificent gesture of giving...very unselfish."

"Well, thank you, Mr. Jingles."

Munching on their hot dogs and sipping their hot chocolate, they continued their conversation, talking about school, what Mary wanted to be when she grew up, and an assortment of other topics. Jacob didn't share much about himself.

"I wish I had you as my grandpa," Mary told him.

"Oh, I'm sure your grandpa is a fine man. Does he live here in the city?"

"My grandpa's dead."

"Oh, Mary, I'm so sad to hear that."

"That's okay. I never really knew him. He lived far away from here." Mary became silent, then said, "Since I don't have a grandfather, can I adopt you as my grandpa?"

A feeling of exultation rushed into Jacob's heart, causing him to smile.

"Certainly. It would be my honor."

"Let's shake on it."

Jacob grasped Mary's delicate little hand and they gave each other an animated shake.

"I have a better idea. Come over here." Jacob gave Mary a big hug.

"I love you, Grandpa."

"I love you, too, Mary."

"We better get back outside."

Jacob called out to Mabel, "How much do I owe you?"

"It's on the house, Mr. Jingles," she said, letting him know she'd overheard their conversation.

"Oh, you don't have to do that. I'll gladly pay."

"Nope. Santa and his helpers eat here for free."

"Well...thank you very much."

Jacob and Mary put on their coats and gloves and went back outside to the kettle.

"That lady was nice," Mary said as she picked up her tin can.

"You better run along now. Your mother and father will be worried about you. I really appreciate your help."

"I'll see you tomorrow, Grandpa."

An emptiness came over Jacob as he watched Mary walk away. She'd brought him so much warmth on this cold winter day. He watched her until she was out of sight, then resumed ringing his bell, joyfully greeting those who walked by.

* * *

Mary ran all the way home, delighted by her relationship with Jacob and the good things they were doing together. At the dinner table that evening, she told her mother and father more about Jacob.

"Mommy, you know that man I told you about...the one I am helping for the Salvation Army?"

"Yes?"

"He told me he doesn't have a home and that he's poor. He lives at the Salvation Army."

"Does he have a family?"

"I don't know. I didn't ask. We've become best friends. I like him so much, I have adopted him as my grandpa. We even shook on it. He's a nice man, Mommy. Sometimes he even lets me ring the bell."

"That's very nice of you, Mary. It is good to help the poor and to make friends with a kind old man who is trying to help others."

* * *

The next morning, Jacob strolled up the street with his kettle and discovered that Mary was waiting for him. "Wow, you certainly are an early bird."

"Haven't you heard…the early bird catches the worm." They both laughed.

Mary, eager to get started, fiddled with her tin coffee can.

"You set up here. I'll go up the street to the other corner and collect some money in my can."

"Okay, boss." Jacob smiled.

Word spread that Mary was helping Jacob. This moved people to give to Mary, knowing it would all be put into Jacob's kettle. Mary made numerous trips back to see Jacob and to empty her can into the kettle.

"Tomorrow, I'm going to have to bring a bigger can," Mary said as she emptied more money into the kettle.

That evening she told her parents about how much fun she was having helping "Mr. Jingles" collect money for the poor.

Her mom and dad sat proudly listening to Mary cheerfully discuss her newfound friend and their joint efforts to collect money for the Salvation Army. Mary wanted to do more. She organized a fund-raiser among her neighbors, family, friends, and relatives, going door to door with her coffee can to collect for the bell ringing campaign. Her first contribution came from her father, a whopping ten-dollar bill, launching her endeavor in an extraordinary way.

Mary wrestled with the weight of the can on her walk to meet Jacob. When she arrived at the street corner with her abundance, Jacob was astonished. He helped her empty the cash into the kettle, not quite able to fully comprehend how a girl of her young age could muster this much interest in such an undertaking. Between the two of them, the collections accumulated so fast that he and Mary were forced to make several trips a day back to the Salvation Army Mission to empty his kettle, astounding everyone there.

After helping Jacob, Mary went home, where her mother was vigorously scrubbing the kitchen floor.

Mary asked, "Can I bring Mr. Jingles home with me for supper one night so you can meet him?"

Her mother, preoccupied with her work and only half listening, said, "Sure." The following morning, Mary met Jacob at his collection point. As he rang his bell, she invited him to supper that evening.

"Oh, I don't know. What would your mommy and daddy think?"

"I asked my mommy and she said it was okay."

Jacob paused for a minute. The offer sounded inviting, but he didn't know what to say.

"Please," Mary begged.

"Well, I suppose if it is all right with your mommy and daddy, it would be okay. I would really like to meet them. Are you sure it's all right?"

"Sure I'm sure."

After they'd finished collecting donations that day, Mary accompanied Jacob to the mission to turn in the kettle. Then, they went off to Mary's house for Jacob to meet her parents and for supper.

Mary burst through the kitchen door, tugging on Jacob's hand, leading him into the house. "Come on in, Mr. Jingles. Here he is, Mommy!" Her anticipation of a warm welcome for her friend was squelched just as soon as her mom laid eyes on Jacob.

Standing there in her kitchen holding her daughter's hand was Jacob McCallum... her estranged father. Emma's face reddened with anger, her nostrils flared, and she began to hyperventilate, tears gushing down her cheeks.

Jacob, equally stunned, dropped Mary's hand, his chest pounding like a kettle drum. His futile search for Emma was over as she materialized before him, an unlikely outcome to his chance meeting of a charming little girl with such a big heart. A gratified look flitted across his face. He stood in front of Emma, nervous yet hopeful that she would run over to embrace him. He had waited so long for this very moment. "Emma?" Jacob said sheepishly with a slight smile.

Her eyes widened as she tried in vain to blink back her tears. "Dad? How dare you!"

Mary looked confused. She was just a baby when she last saw her grandfather, and she had no recollection of him. Her mother told her that he'd passed away. Jacob had had no earthly idea that Mary was his *real* granddaughter. Only by a strange coincidence did Jacob and Emma stand face-to-face. Jacob's prayers had been answered. Emma's nightmare had come true.

"How dare you use my daughter to weasel your way back into my life? How dare you!"

"But, Emma, you don't understand, I had no way of knowing—"

"I understand perfectly!" she interrupted. "You think after all you've done, you can come waltzing back into my life and expect me to embrace you with open arms?"

"But I—"

"Shut up. Don't even talk to me. Get out of my house. Out!"

"This is my real grandpa? But you said he was dead."

"As far as I'm concerned, he is!" Emma shouted as she glared angrily at Jacob.

"Grandpa, don't leave. I love you."

"I love you, too, my child, but I must go. Your mother doesn't want me here."

Hearing the commotion, Emma's husband, Nathaniel, entered the room. He recognized Jacob as the man he'd treated in the hospital weeks before. "What's going on?"

Emma was on a rampage. Mary was crying hysterically. She attempted to run to the door to be with Jacob, but her mother restrained her.

"Out!" Emma demanded as she pointed to the door.

"Don't go, Grandpa," Mary pleaded.

Jacob sadly turned and walked out the door. The next thing

he knew he was standing on the sidewalk in front of the house. He could still hear the shouting coming from within.

"What is it? What's all the commotion?" Nathaniel asked.

"That was my father. I hate him!"

"I love my grandpa. I want to go with him. He's sad," Mary said between sobs.

"I never want you to see him again!"

"But why, Mommy? What did he do?"

"Never mind, Mary. Go to your room."

Mary ran upstairs to her room, crying. Emma stood in the middle of the kitchen as her rage turned to sobs. Nathaniel grabbed her by her arms. She was inconsolable and shaking uncontrollably. "Emma, get a hold of yourself. Calm down and tell me what's wrong."

"I've told you about my father. I can't believe he showed up here after all these years."

"That was your father?"

"Yes."

"That was the man I treated at the hospital . . . the bell ringer. Obviously, he's a changed man. Why don't you at least give him a chance? He's done so much good here in Baltimore."

"I've told you what he's done to my family."

"Yes, but that was years ago. He's been searching for you. Perhaps he wants your forgiveness."

"I will never forgive him for what he has done."

"You didn't even give him a chance to ask for forgiveness. Think about what you are doing. Think of Mary."

"Whose side are you on anyway?"

"It's not a matter of sides. He's your father. He's come a long way to find you. Can't you see by the sheer coincidence of this that it may be God's way of reuniting both of you? And what about Mary? Are you going to deny her the opportunity to know her grandfather?"

"Yes! Yes, I am!"

"Don't be so selfish."

"Selfish? You know what he's done to me. He killed my mother!"

"Yes. You've told me many times. But still..."

"I don't want that man in my life, or Mary's, either."

"Won't you think about it, Emma?"

"I have thought about it; for years I have thought about it."

"But time has a way of changing people."

"That man is evil. He could never change."

"Emma. At least give him a chance."

"I will not!"

Mary was at the top of the stairs, choking back tears, as she listened to her parents argue. She gathered her courage and walked down the steps into the kitchen.

"Are you mad at me, Mommy?"

"No, child, I'm not mad at you, but you stay away from that man. Do you hear me?"

"But he's my grandfather...your daddy. And he's my friend."

"I still don't want you to go near him."

"But, Mommy, I don't understand. When I told you about him in the beginning, you said how nice it was for me to help this poor old man. Now I find out he is my grandpa and you want me to stay away from him. How can that be the right thing to do? I love him."

"That was before I knew he was my father."

"Listen to yourself, Emma," Nathaniel said. "He's your father. Give him a chance to make things better between you."

"He doesn't deserve another chance."

* * *

Brokenhearted, Jacob saw the answer to his prayers slip right through his fingers. Jacob discovered that finding forgiveness could be tenuous. Walking aimlessly around the streets of Baltimore, he tried to make sense of what had just transpired. On his way, he passed several taverns. Did his answer lie within their walls? Would a stiff drink quench his thirst for love and forgiveness? He rationalized that, at the very least, it would offer him an easy escape from the unfathomable pain he was feeling. He checked his pockets for any cash left from the small stipend he received for doing chores around the mission. Did he have enough money to tie one on? He did!

Throwing open the door of a decrepit saloon, he charged toward the bar.

"Can I help you, sir?" the bartender asked.

"Just give me a minute."

Jacob's chest was constricting, making it difficult to breathe. A patron walked over and touched his arm. "Are you okay?"

"Yes, I just need to catch my breath."

"What would you like to drink?" the bartender asked again.

Jacob surveyed the selection behind the bar, then he ordered a glass of vodka.

"Coming right up."

Suddenly, he panicked. A cold sweat rolled down his forehead. Before getting served, he ran out of the bar and continued running down the street until he could run no more. Leaning against the side of a building, he slid down into a sitting position. He grasped his head and surrendered to his fervent urge to cry. *That was a close call*, he said to himself. It had been a long time since he'd craved a drink. He knew he was awfully close to a relapse and it scared him. Reflecting on his surprise meeting with Emma, he realized his hopes of gaining her forgiveness were forever shattered, causing him to irrationally have regrets about his first encounter with Mary. But he treasured the time he'd spent with her, and the agony of never seeing her again haunted him.

Jacob got up and continued his walk. He headed for the rail yard to hop a freight to anywhere...anywhere but Baltimore. As he arrived, he could hear the familiar whistles of the trains coming and going. He sat on the tracks, contemplating which boxcar to board. The thought even crossed his mind to lie down on the tracks and wait for a passing train to run over him, but he decided otherwise. Climbing into a vacant boxcar, he settled in, waiting for it to pull out for parts unknown, not really caring about its destination. The train began to move slowly out of the yard as Jacob watched the lights of the Baltimore skyline pass lazily by. Thoughts raced through his mind about all he had accomplished there, and it suddenly occurred to him that he was throwing it all away. He reminisced about Howard and Bob and all they had done for him...about all he'd learned from them. The lights of the city blurred through his emerging tears.

No! I'm not going to throw my life away again. Jacob jumped from the boxcar while the train was still creeping out of the yard. Hitting the ground hard, he stumbled, twisting his ankle. Hobbling, he headed for the mission. His limp brought back thoughts of Tom. The intermittent stops he made along the way to rest his ankle made his journey back to the mission take several hours, and he arrived late into the night.

"Where have you been, Jacob? It's late. I've been worried about you. Why are you limping?" Bob asked.

"It's a long story, Bob. I'll tell you later. There is something more important we need to talk about. Something terrible has happened."

"What is it?"

"You know how badly I wanted to find Emma, to ask for her forgiveness?"

"Yes."

"Well...tonight it happened."

"But where? How?"

"Remember that little girl I've been telling you about?"

"Mary?"

"Yes. As it turns out, she's my granddaughter."

"What?"

"She took me to her house for supper tonight, and to meet her parents. When I got inside, I discovered that her mother was Emma."

"Oh, wow!"

"Needless to say, our reunion didn't go so well."

"What happened?"

"Let's just say she wasn't so glad to see me. She threw me out and said she never wanted to see me again. She also forbade me from seeing Mary."

"I'm so sorry. How can I help?"

"I don't know if you can. What can you possibly do?"

"Jacob, this is more than a mere coincidence. I think God has had a hand in all of this."

"Then why did it turn out this way?"

"I can't tell you that. You must be patient and have faith."

"I've got some thinking to do. I think I'll go to the chapel for a while and pray on this."

"That's probably a good idea."

* * *

Jacob reluctantly toted his kettle to the corner of Charles and Light Streets. He stood there slowly ringing his bell, constantly staring down the street, hoping to see his granddaughter running up to greet him. It didn't happen. He realized that it never would.

After about two hours, Bob came by to check on him.

"Jacob! How's it going?"

"My heart is just not in it today."

"Why don't you go back to the mission? I'll ring the bell for you."

"Will you? Thanks, Bob. I don't think I can make it through the day out here."

"Why don't you tell me where Emma lives and I'll pay her a visit to see if I can patch things up."

Jacob gave Bob directions to Emma's house and then went back to the mission. After finishing for the day, Bob took the kettle back to be tallied, then he headed out to pay Emma a visit. Nervously, he approached the front door and knocked. Emma answered.

"Hello, I'm Pastor Bob Parsley from the Salvation Army Mission."

"Hello, Pastor, my husband speaks very highly of you. Come on in."

"I'm here about your father."

Emma frowned, feeling a bit uncomfortable. Perhaps even a little guilty. She cocked her head at an angle and her lips tightened, wondering at the purpose for the pastor's visit. A worried look abruptly appeared on her face.

"Is he ill or something?"

"No, but he's heartbroken. He's staying at the Salvation Army Mission and he has been searching for you for a long time to ask for your forgiveness."

"Do you know what he has done to me and my family?"

"Yes, he told me all about it. He's a changed man, Emma, and he would like you to give him the opportunity to make things up to you. He wants a relationship with you and his granddaughter, Mary."

"Well, that's impossible. Not after all he's done."

"Forgiveness is never impossible."

"I'm afraid it is in this case."

"Emma, your father has come a long way to speak with you and he desperately wants to resume his relationship with Mary. He's totally transformed into a new man, not the one you remember, and one exceptionally worthy of your forgiveness. His struggles with alcohol are behind him. You have no idea of the hell he's been through and what he has been able to overcome. Because of him, our bell ringing campaign this year is more successful than ever. What he has been able to do has made a real difference to the needy people of this city."

"Pastor Parsley, I appreciate what you are trying to do, but I just can't subject myself or my daughter to more of the hurt he has inflicted upon us."

"Mary seems to want a relationship with him."

"Yes, but Mary doesn't understand his past."

"Sometimes we should look at situations through the innocent eyes of children. If we do, we come away with a whole new perspective."

"Well, I'm sorry. I don't want to see my father, and I certainly don't want him around Mary."

"Do you believe in forgiveness?"

"Of course."

"Well, then..."

"I can forgive, but I can't forget."

"That's all he wants from you... forgiveness. He understands the difficulty you will encounter forgetting many of the things he has done. Will you please give him another chance?"

Emma carefully considered what Pastor Bob said to her. Then, defiantly, she spoke. "I really don't want to discuss this any further. Is there anything else?"

"No, that is the reason for my visit."

"Well, good day."

"Please, won't you reconsider?"

"No!"

When Bob returned to the mission, he found Jacob lying on his cot, his feet propped up, reading the newspaper. From the pastor's expression, he could discern that Bob's visit with Emma hadn't gone well. Jacob sat upright, swinging his feet over the side of the cot. Bob sat down next to him.

"I paid Emma a visit this evening."

"And?"

"She refuses to see you, or to let Mary see you."

"I was afraid that would be the case. What am I going to do?"

"Wait, Jacob. Just wait. Have faith and things will work out."

"I'm beginning to lose faith. I've tried so hard to make things right. I have changed the way I live my life. I have gone out of my way to help others. What else can I do?"

"I know you have, Jacob."

"Emma refuses to talk to me and now I have lost Mary...the little girl who brought so much happiness into my life."

"Don't give up on it just yet. I know Emma's giving deep thought to what I said. Give her some time to come around. I have faith that she will. In her heart, she knows it's the right thing to do."

Jacob's eyes focused on his feet as they shuffled back and forth on the wooden floor while he solemnly listened to the details of Bob's visit with Emma. Bob felt regret for having to deliver the news to Jacob. He could see the disappointment in his expression as Jacob dismally gazed at the floor. Unable to think of anything uplifting to say, he pondered for a moment. Then...

"I've got another trick up my sleeve."

Encouraged, Jacob looked over at him.

"What are you going to do?"

"As it turns out, she is married to Dr. Brown, the doctor at the hospital who stitched up your head. I think I'll go have a talk with him."

"I thought I recognized him at Emma's house, but I wasn't sure. I knew I had seen him before."

"I'll pay him a visit tomorrow and see if he can help us."

★ ★ ★

The next morning Bob went to the hospital. He waited about two hours until Dr. Nathaniel Brown could see him.

"Pastor Bob? What a pleasant surprise."

"Do you have a few minutes? There's something important I need to speak with you about."

"Yes, I have some time."

"I'm here to talk about Jacob."

"Wow. What a messy situation."

"It sure is."

"What can I do?"

"Jacob has been on a long and bumpy journey to find his children and reconcile with them. I know that in the past, he has done some hurtful things to his family. But he's a changed man. He desperately wants to speak with Emma about her forgiving him. He wants a relationship with her and Mary."

"I read the wonderful article about him in the newspaper. Sounds like he's doing a lot of magnificent things. But that's a very touchy subject with Emma."

"I realize that. If only she would give him a chance. He deserves that, at the very least. He's worked very hard at changing his life. He even had me baptize him! Jacob has made a huge difference at the Salvation Army, and in the city of Baltimore for that matter."

"I remember meeting him for the first time when he came in here and I stitched up his head. He seemed like a colorfully nice fellow. A bit lost, nonetheless."

"Jacob is a special person. He just needs another chance. That is all he wants. I'm afraid he may go back to his old ways if he doesn't get it. That would be a terrible loss."

Nathaniel thought for a second, running his hand through his thick black hair. "I understand." Hesitating, he pressed his lips together. "I'll talk with Emma about this tonight, but I can't promise anything. You know how angry she is about all of this."

"Just do what you can. We'll meet tomorrow at about this time if that's convenient for you?"

"That will be fine."

* * *

Emma was in the kitchen when Nathaniel got home. He entered the back door, hiding his hand behind his back to conceal the delicate bouquet of flowers he'd purchased along the way. As Emma greeted him, he revealed the gift.

"Oh, Nathaniel, they're beautiful. Thank you so much." She rose on her tiptoes and kissed him on the cheek. "You know I love flowers."

"Where's Mary?"

"She's up in her room, brooding."

"She's hurt, Emma. She doesn't understand all of this."

"She will someday."

"No. Don't rob her of the memory of her grandfather."

"She has no memory of him."

"They struck up a close relationship when she was helping him raise money for the Salvation Army."

"She didn't even know he was her grandfather at that time."

"Yes, but that doesn't take away from the fact that they love each other. He loves her, as he does you. And now she knows that the kind old gentleman she came to love is actually her grandfather."

"What does she know? She only spent a short time with him."

"But it was a very special time for her."

"What's your point, Nathaniel?"

"I received a visit from Bob Parsley this afternoon."

"I can only guess as to the subject of that conversation," Emma said sarcastically.

"He said your father has changed. He's been baptized and is doing good deeds in service to mankind. I'd like to talk with you about giving your father a chance at forgiveness."

"Oh, that's what the flowers were all about!" Emma said dismissively as she tossed them on the counter.

"No. The flowers are about how much I love you."

"Nathaniel, I cannot forgive my father for what he has done. I just can't. I have told you this many times before."

"I realize it will be hard for you. This is an opportunity for you to release the anger you have been harboring for all these years. That can only be good for you. Put it to rest. Leave it behind, and start anew. If not for yourself... then do it for Mary."

Emma began to cry. "You don't understand. He never did anything to you. He never broke your heart."

"I'm able to look at this more objectively. I have a fresher perspective than you."

"Your perspective has been spared the heartache and disappointment I have experienced at the hands of my father. So your perspective is through rose-colored glasses."

"Come on, Emma. Please be reasonable."

Nathaniel and Emma began to argue. Mary listened as their voices drifted up the stairs and into her room. She cracked the door to better hear what they were saying. Mary couldn't understand her mother's reluctance to embrace her grandfather. It went against all that Mary had been taught by her parents. As she listened, she began to cry. She tried to contain herself, so as not to alert her parents that she was aware of their arguing. After composing herself, she sneaked down the stairs for a closer look at what was happening in the kitchen, reaching the bottom just as her parents' disagreement ended.

Mary witnessed her mother and father embracing. Her mother was crying as her father tried to soothe her. "I love you, Emma."

"You can't comprehend how I feel toward my father." Emma's weeping became more intense.

"Yes, I can. I understand how you feel, and why you feel that way. His actions have impacted your life in many negative ways. I can't say that I blame you for feeling the way you do."

"Then why do you want me to give him another chance to break my heart?"

"Because I believe in forgiveness."

"I believe in forgiveness, too. But my father is beyond it."

"Oh, and who appointed *you* the one who determines who is forgiven and who's not?"

"You know what I mean."

"No. I don't know what you mean. You owe it to your father to show him some compassion and forgiveness. He's paid the price."

"And what do you know about the price he's paid? He hasn't paid me anything. In fact, he owes me! He owes me the life of my mother, my lost childhood, and much more than you will ever understand."

Nathaniel grasped Emma by the arms and looked down at her compassionately. "I didn't mean it that way. What I mean is...he's come here to give back much of what he has taken from you. Just give him a chance."

Mary walked into the kitchen, her eyes red from crying, dried tears staining her face.

"Mommy, please...please forgive my grandpa."

"Mary, go back up to your room. Your father and I are talking."

Mary glared at her mother, before turning and running up the stairs.

"No, Mary...wait!" her father called out to her.

Mary stopped, turning to face her mother and father, then timidly reentered the kitchen.

"Nathaniel! What are you doing? I told her to go to her room so we could discuss this."

"This has as much to do with her as it does us. We need to listen to how Mary feels."

Befuddled and not knowing what to do, she stood there quietly. There was a conspicuous silence in the room as they all looked at each other, wondering who would speak first. Nathaniel took the initiative. "Mary? How do you feel about what is happening?"

"I don't like to see you and Mommy arguing. I don't understand why Mommy doesn't love her father. He's a nice man. He's my best friend, my grandpa...and I love him. I want him to come and live with us."

"That's impossible, child!"

"Now, Emma, give her a chance to say her piece."

"When I met him, he was Mr. Jingles. We became best friends. He was so nice to me, and he taught me about giving, and how good it makes you feel. Then, the most wonderful thing happened..." Mary began to cry.

"What is it, love?" her father asked.

"I learned that Mr. Jingles is my grandpa, too. That made me happy. But Mommy doesn't love Grandpa. She hates him, and I don't know why. She told me he was dead and I believed her for all this time. I love Grandpa and I want to be with him. Please, Mommy, let me see Grandpa. I want to spend Christmas with him."

"Sweetie, you are too young to understand this difficult situation," Emma interjected.

"All I know is that I love Grandpa and I want to spend time with him."

"But, Mary, you don't know what he—"

Nathaniel interrupted, "Why don't you go up to your room for a while so Mommy and Daddy can talk more about this. Will you, my dear?"

"Yes, Daddy."

Mary retreated to her room, but left the door slightly ajar, making it easier to eavesdrop on the conversation. She positioned herself in front of the door.

"Do you see how this has affected Mary?"

"Yes, but I still can't bring myself to forgive that man. And I certainly don't want Mary around him."

"If that's truly how you feel, though I think you are terribly wrong, I'll respect your wishes...but I want you to know that I strongly disagree. I will not be the one to tell Mary. That'll be your job."

★ ★ ★

It was two days before Christmas and snow was falling. Jacob stood on the street corner lethargically ringing his bell. His heart just wasn't in it. The Christmas he'd hoped for with his family was not in the cards. It dampened his spirits and he felt Christmas, from now on, would just be another day to him.

Back at the Brown household, Emma busily prepared for the Christmas Eve feast she planned for the family.

Mary, who had sequestered herself in her room since the events surrounding her grandfather, decided she would ask her mother one more time to change her mind about seeing Jacob.

"Mommy, can I go to the street corner and see Grandpa?"

"No, you may not."

"But why? Why won't you let me see him?"

"We've been through this, Mary. Now, I don't want to talk about it anymore!"

"You're mean!" Mary said as she ran back up the stairs, crying.

Meanwhile, Jacob's bell rang, almost muted against the bustle on the street as people rushed to do their last-minute shopping before the holiday. Jacob's thoughts were preoccupied with images of Mary and Emma and his deep yearning to be with them. The opportunity to spend this special Christmas with those he loved seemed to slip through his fingers. With regularity, he glanced down the street, praying that Mary would come running up with her tin can to help him.

"Jacob? You don't seem like your jolly old self today. What's wrong?" one of his frequent givers asked.

"Just not feeling up to par."

"Sorry to hear that. I hope you're feeling better by Christmas," the man said as he dropped some coins into Jacob's kettle.

"Thank you, Pat."

"Merry Christmas."

"Same to you," Jacob replied in an uncharacteristic, almost inaudible tone.

The gentle snowfall, which greeted the early morning, fell heavily now, quickly accumulating on the streets, sidewalks, and rooftops. The once-crowded streets were almost abandoned, except for a few stragglers still intent on picking up a last-minute Christmas gift before retiring to the warmth and coziness of the indoors. Jacob stubbornly remained, ringing his bell, trying to squeeze the last bit of generosity from those still brave enough to weather the elements.

Still refusing to believe that Mary would no longer be a part of his life, he kept looking up the street where she'd first appeared, hoping against hope that he would see her standing there. The reality of the situation nagged at him, telling him what he already knew . . . that he was only fooling himself. Shaking the snow from his coat and hat, he packed up and began his trek back to the mission.

As he walked through the snowstorm, he heard the faint calling of an angel's voice.

"Grandpa, Grandpa, wait up."

He turned, at first thinking he was hallucinating, dropping his kettle. Mary ran up the sidewalk, catching him in a fervent embrace. He swung her around, a colossal grin on his face. They clung to each other, Mary burying her head in his stomach as they both began to cry.

"I don't understand, Mary. I thought your mother said you could never see me again."

"I ran away to be with you."

"Oh, Mary, you can't do this. Your mom and dad will be in

a panic. And your mom will blame me. I have to take you back home."

"No, Grandpa, I won't go."

"But it's the right thing to do."

"Please, let me stay with you."

"You can't. I'll get into all kinds of trouble."

"I'm not going back home."

"But you have to."

"No, I don't!" Mary took off, running down the street.

Jacob pursued her, calling her name and demanding that she come back, but she escaped him. She rounded the corner and he lost sight of her.

★ ★ ★

Mary's mother discovered the note left behind in Mary's room, stating her intentions to spend Christmas with her grandpa. The last Emma saw of Mary was hours earlier. She assumed she was in her room, brooding. Furious, yet worried, she called Nathaniel at the hospital.

"Nathaniel, Mary's missing."

"What?"

"Mary, she is missing!"

"What do you mean, missing?"

"She's run away to be with my father. She's been gone for hours."

"I'll be right home."

★ ★ ★

Jacob had walked for miles through the vicious snowstorm, searching everywhere—calling out Mary's name. He couldn't find her. Panic-stricken and weary, he began asking the few strangers he passed if they had seen her.

"Have you seen a little girl with a gray coat and red scarf?"

Every answer was the same... *"No, I haven't."*

* * *

Nathaniel arrived home and got the details from Emma.

"He's kidnapped her. I know he has!"

"Emma, I think you're jumping to conclusions."

"No, I'm not. He's stolen our daughter!"

Nathaniel called the police and explained that his daughter had run away and had been missing for hours. He told them that she might be with Jacob, giving descriptions of them both. The police posted an all-points bulletin, and dozens of policemen fanned out in search of them.

"I'll get together some neighbors and go search for her."

"I'm going, too," Emma demanded.

"No, you stay here in case the police call or she comes home."

Nathaniel and his posse began their search. They went to the corner of Charles and Light Streets to see if she was with Jacob. When they arrived, they found Jacob's kettle lying on its side about a hundred feet from his usual place. His bell lay next to it, mostly buried in the snow. Other than that, there was no sign of them.

He's gone. Maybe Emma was right, Nathaniel thought.

He directed the search party to split up and search the city.

* * *

Jacob continued to traipse through the snow, which by now was about a foot deep. He checked the streets, the alleys, looking in buildings and under stairwells. He was running out of hope. *Have faith, Jacob. Have faith*, he kept saying to himself.

Jacob continued to comb the back alleys and side streets. As he labored through the deep snow of an alley, he continued to call her name. "Mary. Mary! Where are you? Maaarrry!" he yelled at the top of his lungs.

"Grandpa, I'm over here." He heard her crying.

There, under a fire escape, he found her huddled, shivering from the cold.

"Mary, I've been looking all over for you. I'm sure everyone else has been searching for you, as well."

"Grandpa, I'm cold but I don't want to go home. Where can we go to get warm?"

"We need to get you back home. Your parents are probably worried sick."

Jacob held her in his coat until she warmed up, then taking her by her hand, they walked from the alley out onto the street. A brisk wind thrust snow in their faces, blinding them. All they could see was a sheet of white. Walking became more difficult, and Mary shivered uncontrollably.

"I'm so tired, Grandpa. I can't walk anymore."

Jacob picked her up in his arms and continued walking. After several blocks he became exhausted, but given the circumstances, he felt compelled to continue. The sensation of a dull pain began in his chest and trickled down his left arm. He ignored it and kept walking. Precipitously, the pain shot through his chest as if he were being stabbed with a dull knife.

"I have to put you down for a while. Do you think you can walk a little bit?"

"I'll try."

Jacob took a few more steps, grabbed his chest, and fell to the ground.

"Grandpa!"

"Go get help. Hurry!"

Mary ran to find someone to help, leaving Jacob lying in the snow. Fortunately, she saw a policeman up the street.

"Mister Policeman!" she screamed. "Help me!"

He ran toward Mary. By the time he reached her, she'd become hysterical, shrieking something about her grandpa. He couldn't make sense of what she said.

"What is it, little girl?"

"It's my grandpa! He's hurt!"

The policeman immediately recognized Mary as the little girl for whom they were searching.

"We've been looking all over for you. Are you all right?"

"Yes, it's my grandpa!"

She led the officer back to where Jacob was now rolling in the snow, writhing in pain.

"Grandpa, I love you!"

Mary fell to her knees to comfort him, but the officer asked her to stand out of the way.

"What is it, sir?" the officer asked.

Between winces, Jacob said, "I think I'm having a heart attack."

The policeman flagged down the car of a fellow officer.

"I need you to get this man to the hospital; he's having a heart attack. This is the man we've been looking for."

The two officers lifted Jacob into the backseat of the squad car, instructing Mary to get in the front seat. The policeman jumped in the driver's side and radioed the precinct where Nathaniel sat with his head in his hands awaiting news about Mary.

He heard the officer's radio call over a speaker in the room.

"We found her. We're en route to the hospital."

The signal faded and the transmission became inaudible. It was unclear whether Mary was injured, but that's how Nathaniel interpreted it. Unsettled, he ran to the desk sergeant and asked to use the telephone to call his wife.

"Get to the hospital right away. They are taking Mary there."

"What happened to her? Is she all right?"

"I don't know. Hurry! I'll meet you there."

Nathaniel and Emma rushed to the hospital, where they found Mary being comforted by an officer.

"Mary, are you all right?" her father asked, his face gripped by terror.

She reached up for her mother and father, who smothered her with hugs.

The officer replied, "She's fine, but I'm afraid her grandfather has had a heart attack."

"Is he going to be okay, Mommy?"

"I'm sure he'll be just fine," she fibbed, careful not to upset Mary even more. The truth was, Emma was filled with worry, as well.

"I'm going up to his room. Do you want to go with me, Emma?" Nathaniel asked.

"No, I'll stay here with Mary."

Cold, and fatigued from her experience, Mary quickly fell asleep in her mother's reassuring arms.

"But he's your father."

Emma gave Nathaniel a stern glare. Not wanting to make a scene, Nathaniel dashed upstairs to see if he could help. Minutes later, Bob Parsley arrived at the hospital and went straight to Jacob's room, where he prayed for his friend.

The news of Jacob's heart attack traveled fast. Flowers and messages flooded the front desk at the hospital. Emma didn't understand how all these people knew her father. The headline in the evening newspaper read, JACOB'S BELL SILENCED BY HEART ATTACK. It was the lead to a feature story dedicated to Jacob and all the good deeds he had done. Emma had no idea her father was such a well-regarded and kind man.

As Jacob lay near death, he received many visitors. Even the mayor stopped by the hospital—mainly for a photo op, as politicians usually do.

"Emma, why don't you go up and see your father? This may be your last chance." Nathaniel pleaded with her.

"Yes, Emma. I think it is time you put all this behind you," Bob Parsley urged.

"But, Pastor Parsley, I'm afraid."

"Nathaniel and I will go with you."

They took off up the stairs leading to Jacob's room. The veracity of the moment hit Emma hard, as she struggled for her breath, running just as fast as she could. When they arrived in Jacob's room, she began to weep upon seeing Jacob lying motionless on the bed, clinging to life. She began second-guessing her rash decision to push her father away when he came to her asking for forgiveness. Why had she been so cruel? Thoughts of Mary's love for her grandfather and the good deeds they'd done together flashed through her mind. As she gazed at her father's still face, she contemplated her reaction to him after he'd knocked at her door. Regrets filled her. "Daddy, I'm so sorry. If I had forgiven you, none of this would have happened." She broke down again.

"Don't blame yourself, Emma. This is not your fault," Bob assured her.

"I just feel this happened because of me."

Moving closer to his bedside, Emma held her father's hand for a moment. Then Bob Parsley led her away from the bed to a corner of the room, where they prayed together.

"Forgive me, Lord, for being so selfish." She abruptly stopped praying and looked at Bob. "I can't believe what I just said. I am asking God to forgive me, yet I refused to forgive my father when he begged me for forgiveness."

"God understands. You're forgiven."

Emma walked back over to Jacob's bedside and gently stroked his forehead.

"Daddy, I forgive you. I forgive you. Can you ever forgive me?"

"I'm sure he already has," Bob said.

The nurse came in and cleared the room. "He needs his rest. You'll all have to leave now."

Emma stared down at her father, wondering if this would be the last time she would see him alive.

* * *

As Jacob lay there drifting in and out of consciousness, he saw the faint images of a man and a woman standing over him. He could barely make out their features.

"Frankie? Amanda?"

Yes, we're here with you," Amanda answered.

"But...but I thought you were..."

"I know, darling," Amanda said.

"Dad, I'm here to say I love you, and that Mom and I forgive you."

"Jacob, I love you with all my heart," Amanda whispered.

"Oh, how I have missed the both of you. I'm so sorry for what I've done."

"You don't have to be sorry anymore."

"Dad, we'll stay here with you as long as we can."

"Can't you stay forever?"

"No, my dear, we can only stay for a while. Now, get some rest."

A nurse entered the room to check on Jacob, having overheard him speaking. Jacob's vision of Amanda and Frankie faded.

"My wife and son...where'd they go? They were just here visiting me."

"Mr. McCallum, you've had no visitors for hours."

"That can't be. I was just talking to them."

"You must have been dreaming. Now why don't you relax and go back to sleep."

★ ★ ★

That evening, Emma called Tom in Chicago.

"Tommy, Daddy had a heart attack."

"Oh, so he paid you a visit, too."

"Tommy, he might die."

"He's been dead for years in my mind."

"He's changed. You wouldn't believe the good deeds he's been doing here in Baltimore. The newspaper has written about him on two occasions. It's almost as if he's a movie star or something. The mayor even came to see him here in the hospital. Will you come, if not for him, for me?"

"I'm sorry, Emma, I can't do that."

"Please."

"Sorry, Emma."

"Won't you reconsider? I've forgiven him. You need to forgive him, too. Please?"

"I can't. I'm sorry."

Emma began to bawl.

Nathaniel took the phone and resumed the conversation.

"Tom? This is Nathaniel. You need to listen. Your father is very ill. He may not make it. Your sister and Mary are distraught, and they need you. And you need to see your father before it's too late. After you learn about his new life, surely you'll be open to forgiving him, as well. I just know it."

There was silence on the phone while Tom considered their request.

"Oh, all right. I'll come, but only for Emma and Mary, not my father."

"For whatever reason, it is important that you be here."

"I'll catch a train first thing in the morning."

"Thank you, Tom. This will mean the world to Emma."

Bob called his friend Howard to tell him about Jacob.

"Oh, no. Do you think he'll make it?"

"They don't know."

"I'll get there just as soon as I can."

"Okay, Howard. Sorry I had to be the bearer of such bad news."

Early the next morning, Christmas Eve, Tom boarded a train bound for Baltimore. Emotionally tormented, he wanted to be there for the sake of Emma and Mary, yet he also regretted not being able to spend Christmas with his family. He would have brought them along, but couldn't afford the fare.

While sitting in the passenger car, a gentleman asked Tom if he could sit down next to him.

"Sure. No problem."

After a few moments Tom glanced over at him.

He looks familiar, he thought to himself. *I've seen him before somewhere, but I don't know where.*

The gentleman next to him was thinking the same of Tom. For about an hour they sat shoulder to shoulder without speaking. Tom rose from his seat and crossed in front of the man seated next to him.

"Excuse me," he said. "I need to use the restroom."

As Tom walked up the aisle, the man left in the seat was drawn to his limp.

"My goodness, that's Tom McCallum," he said aloud.

By coincidence, or divine intervention, Tom and Howard Angel were seated next to each other for the day-long trip to Baltimore to see Jacob.

When Tom returned, Howard stood to allow him easy passage back to his seat. After a few moments had passed, Howard said, "Are you Tom McCallum?"

"Yes, but how did you know that?"

"I am Pastor Howard Angel. I accompanied your father the day he came to see you."

"I thought you looked familiar, but I couldn't place where I met you."

"We never really got a chance to meet. It was a very brief and tension-filled encounter."

"Yeah, my father and I have been on bad terms for years. I guess I was a little hard on him that day."

"I'd say so. Are you aware that your father had a heart attack? I'm on my way to see him."

"So am I."

"That's wonderful."

"I'm not going for his sake, but for my sister's and my niece."

During their journey, Howard began telling Tom about how he met his father and about his magnificent transformation. He told him about the wonderful things he had done in Baltimore, that he was baptized, and that he stopped drinking and smoking. This took Tom by surprise. He couldn't believe there was a good bone in his father's entire body. Hearing all this was a bit humbling. By the trip's end, Tom's opinion of his father had been altered somewhat by the stories Howard told him. But as far as he was concerned, the jury was still out on forgiveness.

It was late evening when they arrived in Baltimore. The weather was cold, but the snow clouds had given way to a star-filled sky and a full moon. Howard and Tom shared a cab to the hospital, where they were greeted warmly.

"Tommy, it's so good to see you," Emma said.

Tom gave his sister a firm embrace. "It's good to see you, too, sis."

Mary came over and stood, looking up at him.

"How's my little Mary? You're growing up."

"Merry Christmas, Uncle Tommy."

"Merry Christmas to you." He turned back to Emma. "How's Dad?" he asked.

"I'm surprised you would ask."

"Howard, Dad's pastor in Chicago, told me about how he has changed and about all the good things he has been doing."

"Hello, Emma. I'm Howard Angel. Your father is a wonderful man."

"So how is he?" Tom asked again.

"He's out of danger and feeling much better. Do you want to go see him?"

A scowl immediately replaced Tom's pleasant expression.

"No. I'll wait down here. Remember, the reason I'm here is for you and Mary."

"Come on, Tommy. Seeing you will make him feel much better, and it will do you some good, as well."

"I'll stay here with Mary. You and Howard go on up."

Emma was disappointed. She'd hoped Tom would be more receptive to seeing their father, and perhaps even forgiving him so that they could all be a family again.

While in the waiting room, Tom wrestled with his feelings. Mary went on and on about her grandfather and how much she loved him. She told Tom about all the fun they had collecting money for the Salvation Army. As he listened, his heart began to soften. The constant flow of visitors into Jacob's room puzzled him. *Everyone seems to love this guy. But why? Could he have actually changed this much?*

When he reached for a newspaper on the table to pass the time, his eyes locked on the article about his father. Curious, he began reading. His face went through a number of expressions as his eyes darted from paragraph to paragraph. When he'd finished reading, he slowly laid the paper on his lap and looked out with a blank stare, a confounded expression on his face. "Well, I'll be..."

Tom's thoughts were interrupted when Pastor Bob approached Mary.

"How's your grandpa?"

"Much better. I can't wait to see him. This is my Uncle Tommy," she said, introducing Tom.

"Tom McCallum. I'm Jacob's son from Chicago," Tom said, offering his hand to Bob.

"Good meeting you. I'm Pastor Bob Parsley. Your dad has been staying with us at the Salvation Army Mission here in Baltimore." Shaking Tom's hand, he continued, "What a fine gentleman your father is. I'm so glad to hear he's doing better. He had us all worried there for a while."

Emma and Howard bounded down the stairs, both smiling.

"How's Grandpa, Mommy?"

"He's in such great spirits."

"When can I see him?"

Mary's question went unanswered as Howard and Bob's reunion took precedence.

"Howard! It's so good to see you."

As they embraced, Howard said, "Good to see you, as well, my old friend. And it's great to hear that Jacob is on the mend."

"That's good news for all of us."

Nathaniel came into the waiting room. He'd just finished making his rounds. Emma introduced her husband to Howard. Nathaniel grasped Tom's hand firmly.

"Great to see you, Tom. When did you get in?"

"Just a while ago."

"Have you seen your father yet?"

Embarrassed, he admitted that he hadn't, making the excuse that he stayed with Mary while Howard and Emma paid their respects. He was caught off-guard by all the adulation his father was receiving. He started to have the feeling that he was missing something. *I need to meet this man*, he thought.

Pulling Emma off to the side, he said, "I think I'm going to go up and visit with Dad for a while."

Astonished, Emma lit up with a broad smile. "I'll go with you."

"Actually, I'd like to go up alone if you don't mind. After all I've heard, there are some important things I need to say to him."

"I understand."

Tom climbed the stairs apprehensively, pondering what he would say to his father. As he entered the room, Jacob looked at him as if he was going to have another heart attack.

"Hello, my son! You are the last person I expected to see."

"Dad, I came to say how sorry I am for misjudging you. You were seeking my forgiveness; now I'm seeking yours. Can you forgive me?"

"No need for me to forgive you. You have done nothing wrong as far as I am concerned. It is *I* who need *your* forgiveness."

Tom began to weep, as did Jacob.

"Dad, I forgive you for everything. I'm so sorry I've treated you so poorly."

"Don't worry about it, Tom. Your forgiveness is more special to me than you could ever imagine. My journey is now complete."

"I just wish that Mom and Frankie could be here with us," Tom told his father.

"They are. They visited me last night. Your mom hasn't changed a bit after all these years."

"But, Dad. That's impossible. They're—"

"I know, son. It must have been a dream."

Jacob's and Tom's sweet reunion was interrupted when Emma, Mary, Howard, and Bob entered the room. Mary, happy to see her grandfather, sprinted over to Jacob and jumped up in the bed.

"Grandpa! I love you so much. I thought you were going to die."

"Don't worry about me. I'm not going anywhere."

They all laughed.

"Uh-oh, here comes the sergeant, Nurse Audrey," Jacob said as he chuckled.

"Sorry, but Mr. McCallum needs his rest. I'm going to have to kick you all out of here. Besides, children aren't even supposed to be in here. You can visit him again tomorrow afternoon," she said, not unkindly.

* * *

On Christmas Day, Jacob's room was overflowing with family and friends. They even managed to sneak Mary in again to see him. This made the day extra special for both of them. Christmas music played quietly on the radio Emma brought.

"Emma?"

"Yes, Dad?"

"Since I wasn't around, and didn't get to dance with you at your wedding, I was wondering if you would honor me with a dance."

Emma became emotional. "I would be honored."

Tom and Howard helped Jacob to his feet. He reached out and brought Emma to his chest. As they danced, there wasn't a dry eye in the room. Toward the end of the song, Mary joined in, wrapping her arms around both of them.

The room filled with well-wishers. Nurse Audrey turned a blind eye—not that she could have controlled the situation anyhow. Later in the day, Bob Parsley arrived.

"Merry Christmas. Here's a gift for you," he said to Jacob.

"Bob, you didn't have to go and do that."

"Shush...and open it," he said, laughing.

The box was wrapped neatly with an attractive bow. Jacob looked bewildered. He opened the accompanying card, staring at its cover. Then, he read it aloud. *"You can't forgive without love, nor can you love without forgiveness."* Turning the page, he continued reading. *"Forgiveness can never change the past, but it can certainly change the future. We all hope you enjoy a bright future with your new friends and family. Merry Christmas!"*

Jacob grew serious, looking around the room at the friends and family that surrounded him, his eyes moist. "How am I ever going to thank all of you?"

The subdued interlude was lightened as Mary yelled, "Open your present, Grandpa!"

The room exploded in laughter.

"Okay. Okay!" Jacob replied, grinning from ear to ear.

He carefully unwrapped the gift.

"What is it?" Mary asked.

Her mother touched her on the shoulder. "Be patient."

Jacob removed the gift from the box, revealing the bell he'd rung on the streets of Baltimore with so much love and enthusiasm. Bob had retrieved it from the snow the day Mary went missing. Jacob couldn't resist and he began ringing it. After a few rings, he stopped and looked at the side of the bell. He discovered that Bob had had it engraved—JACOB'S BELL. He laughed out loud and proceeded to ring it as loud as he could. Spontaneously, those in the room began putting money in the gift box. Even the nurses and doctors in the hospital came in the room to give. The box overflowed as money fell out onto the bed. Emma and Tom looked at each other, contented. Nurse Audrey stood in the corner, her arms crossed over her chest, shaking her head while smiling at Jacob. Jacob looked at her and gave her a wink.

* * *

Through the innocent eyes of a child, Jacob was not judged. Mary saw him as a generous and compassionate man who gave lovingly of himself to help others. She was blind to Jacob's transgressions and did not persecute him for his past. Because of what Mary witnessed, Jacob's children were able to see a new man in their father—a man born again out of a tragic past, a man freed from guilt and now forgiven. Oh, what a glorious day this was for Jacob McCallum.

Jacob fully recovered and took up residence with Emma and her family. His relationship with his children and Mary blossomed into a wonderful and fulfilling kinship. He and Mary were inseparable. Jacob, with the help of his granddaughter, continued his work with Bob Parsley and the Salvation Army as each Christmas season approached. Christmas of 1944 was the best day of Jacob's life, for on this day he received the true gift of forgiveness. He lived happily for another six years before his heart failed him, and his soul was reunited with Amanda and Frankie.

Jacob has been gone for almost seventy years now, but his bell still sits atop his Bible on a bookshelf in the family home, now occupied by Mary, her daughter, and three grandchildren. Jacob's Bell could never be silenced, though, because he rang it with such love and compassion. Each Christmas, thousands of bells, just like Jacob's, ring to remind us that Christmas is a time for giving... and a time for forgiving.

To this day in Baltimore, in the still of December's night air, if one listens carefully, the faint ringing of Jacob's Bell can be heard in the distance.